CHAINING

daisy

ANN

DENTON

Cover by *Book Brander Boutique*

Le Rue
Publishing

Le Rue Publishing
320 South Boston Avenue, Suite 1030
Tulsa, OK 74103
www.LeRuePublishing.com
ISBN: 978-1-951714-33-8

To my muse. Thanks for interrupting my writing schedule with this novella that spun out of control.

AUTHOR'S NOTE

This book contains a taboo romance with a stepfather-stepdaughter relationship, Daddy kink, a consensual Dom/sub dynamic, spanking, somnophilia, explicit sex and language, and other content that may be triggering. There is no cheating or other woman drama in this book.

GUNNAR

*T*he hospital hallway is too bright for my mood. Surgery just went wrong for a patient and my gut twists sourly over it. I fucking hate when I lose someone. My fingers clench.

I sigh, recalling the wife's face when I told her that her husband didn't make it. *Fuck. The guy couldn't have been over fifty.* I spent more time studying the location of his tumor and surrounding blood vessels than his age, but it still bugs me that I can't recall it. I'm certain they had kids, but she hadn't brought them in with them ... of course, it was an emergency surgery. Now, the kids won't get to say goodbye.

Goddammit. They trusted me to be the best. I was supposed to be the best.

It doesn't help my mood that I was called out of bed at three in the morning and was in the O.R. until seven. My stomach is now demanding food, even if that means vending machine fare because the hospital cafeteria doesn't open for another hour.

At least the floor is mostly quiet right now. Visitors usually come after work, not early in the morning. Patients are grabbing what little sleep they can between pokings and proddings. I'm probably headed back to bed for a bit after I dictate my notes and relive my failure—trying to suss out what went wrong.

My body itches to get to the gym, to lift weights, to expel this negative energy darting around inside my chest and regain some control. Yes, a good gym session first, and then I'll obsessively dive into articles on the tumor I just attempted to extract—like a quarterback trying to determine their opponent's weaknesses, only with much higher stakes.

I reach the alcove with the vending machines only to find someone already there. Someone in fuzzy pink socks that hug her shapely calves, striped pink sleep shorts, and a soft gray t-shirt. Brunette hair is gathered into a messy bun on top of her head that has flyaways escaping every which way.

My throat dries out at the soft expanse of exposed skin from the woman's legs, which are pale and creamy, as if they've hardly seen the sun. The shorts cling to the curve of her ass and I think about the term my surgical assistant used the other day when the young idiot talked about his latest conquest. Cake. That ass is pure cake.

I stand behind the woman, who's clearly an overnight visitor in the ward, gawking like a pervert and inhaling the scent of her citrusy shampoo.

I'm struck dumb just by the shape of her, which is odd. No, not just odd. Stupid. At forty, I've had more women than I can count. I haven't even seen this woman's face yet. *What's wrong with me?*

Sleep deprivation. That must be it.

Or maybe it's the fact that my recertification boards are coming up and I've been studying instead of getting laid. I need to go home and jerk off before I go to sleep.

I scrub a hand down my face, telling myself to snap out of it. But that lush ass atop those perfect thighs keeps drawing my eyes like a magnet.

She must sense me, because the woman turns around.

And if I thought her ass took me out, her face destroys me. A couple of freckles dotted over a pert little nose, thick lips, soft thin brows, and big blue eyes lined with dark lashes— and young. The woman is young. Twenties maybe.

Utterly gorgeous.

She smiles up at me without any guile, not flirty or seductive, just genuine and shiny as a penny. And nowadays, since no one uses pennies anymore and everyone's nose is always in their phones instead of giving out friendly greetings, that sort of glinting smile is utterly rare. Seeing it makes me feel like I just found a lucky coin.

"You can go first if you want. I haven't decided." Her voice is soft and quiet, like she's shy.

My body and mind instantly react to her speaking by bombarding me with a million reactions at once. *I love the cadence of her voice. The breathy quality. I wonder if she's breathy in bed. Is she even legal? Do I care? Of course I care. Because I have to. God, she'd better be legal.*

What she's wearing should be illegal.

My eyes travel down over the thin, worn gray t-shirt she's wearing, which has two little cartoon eyelids with eyelashes closed and the word "Goodnight" written under them in script. It's so innocent that I don't even know why it turns me on so much but it does. I can't tell if she's wearing a bra or not and wondering instantly sets me off.

But then I realize I'm probably coming across as a creep. A total perv. *Fuck, I need to get some sleep and I sure as shit need to stop staring at her.*

I tear my eyes away from her chest and look over at the vending machine. "What are you thinking about getting, so I don't grab the last one?" I go for gentlemanly, my words contrasting the filthy images running through my head.

This alcove is out of sight of other people. If I knew her—if we were together—I could shove her up against one of the vending machines and have my hand down those silky shorts in under a minute. I wish I fucking knew her.

"I'm trying to decide if I want a candy bar or something like Skittles." She tosses a single-shoulder shrug my way.

I shake my head, words pouring out of my mouth before I can stop them and decide if they're a good idea or not. "So, sugar or sugar? No trail mix? No energy bar? Nothing healthy at all?"

She rolls those gorgeous blue eyes of hers. "Ok, Daddy."

The retort is supposed to be sarcastic but it makes my cock thicken. Fuck.

What is happening right now?

My throat closes up as I watch her pop her hip to the side tauntingly and notice how the move makes the pink fabric creep up, nearly revealing the globes of her ass.

"Want to tell me to make my bed and be home by nine too?" she sasses, that shy first impression she gave me fizzling away.

God yes I do. My home. My bed. Except instead of making my bed I want her *in* it at nine every night.

"How old are you?" I ask, taking a step closer, feeling the air between us sizzle, all my tiredness and hunger forgotten, transformed into this burning curiosity. I resist the urge to touch her soft skin, to put a hand on her shoulder and see if I can feel a bra strap under her shirt. Too soon, I tell myself. "I wouldn't think anyone over the age of twelve would want pure sugar and chemical crap for breakfast," I add, trying to tack on a reason for my question that has nothing to do with my hardening dick. God, she better be of age. If not, I'm turning around right this second.

"I'm eighteen—" Her arms cross defensively and that adorable little mouth is still open to insult me further, I'm sure, but I interrupt her, trying not to let my relief that she's legal turn into a giddy grin.

"Well then, I guess I can let you have a curfew that's a little later than nine. But if you aren't home by ten-thirty sharp ..." I cut myself off, nearly biting my tongue. I want so badly to say I will take her over my knee and spank her.

But what the fuck is this? We aren't in some step daddy porn video. No one but a creep says that shit in real life. Right?

Still, it takes everything I have to hold it back because the image pops up so clearly and easily in my mind. I'm sitting on my bed, and she walks in hesitantly, wearing the very thing she has on now. I wave her over, and she shuffles timidly to me, knowing she's in trouble. Her cute face is repentant, but she doesn't beg because she knows it won't do any good. I order her up, and she crawls across the mattress until she's positioned above my lap on all fours. I press a hand to the small of her back and gently lower her onto my thighs, belly down. Then I carefully slide down her pajama shorts and panties until the round globes of her ass appear before me … fuck my life. I'm a pervert. Where the hell is this kink coming from?

"You gonna ground me, old man?"

Fuck. Does she think I'm old? Disgusting? My boner deflates and so does some other internal part of me, one I've never felt before—it makes my chest grow tight. "I'm not old."

"You've got to be, what, like sixty?"

Horror flies through my stomach. I work out four times a week. I might not have a six-pack, but I'm no slouch in any other department. At six foot one, I'm tall and in good shape. I have a little salt and pepper in my brown hair and some crow's feet around my eyes, but damn. "Have you ever even met anyone over the age of twenty-five? Fuck's sake, I'm only forty. You just ruined my morning."

"Not your whole week? Bummer. That's what I was shooting for." She gives me a naughty grin and a wink.

"You little brat." I shake my head in disbelief but that tight feeling in my chest eases and something swoops around inside my stomach. She's teasing me. This hot woman is teasing me.

She giggles and the sound is so sweet and carefree it nearly knocks me back a step.

"Why are you here in the hallway harassing old men to begin with?" I ask her.

The smile stiffens on her face and turns into something stilted and sad. "It's my mom." Her head jerks in the direction of one of the doors down the hall as her lips press together into a thin line. Even though I see that kind of look, that careworn worry, that frayed hope, every single day—even though I'm used to it—I absolutely can't stand to see that expression on her face.

That's when I reach out and put a hand on her shoulder. I don't let myself put it on top to feel for the bra strap because that wouldn't be right. And even if I am a perv, I'm not a sleazy one. I place my palm on the side, just barely cupping her shirt.

"We'll do our best to take care of her," I promise.

Whatever willpower she was using to mask her fear slips and this vulnerable, unguarded expression comes over her. Tears fill her eyes, and she nods, avoiding my gaze, trying to keep from crying because she's probably got to walk back in there soon, and she doesn't want her mom to see.

"I'm Doctor Strong." I drop her shoulder and hold out my hand, cursing myself internally for stiffening up and becoming so formal, but what else am I supposed to do?

"No. No way. That is not your name." She sheds her sadness for suspicion, eyeing my hand.

"Um ... yes, it is." I've never gotten this reaction before. I start to fold in my fingers and retract the hand. Apparently, she's going to leave me hanging.

She rolls her eyes and wedges her tiny fingers between mine for a split second to shake. Electricity lights me up at her touch even though it only lasts an instant and she's pulling away a moment later. "Seriously? Strong?"

"Yes. Seriously."

"If you tell me your first name is Richard or Peter, I'm going to scream."

I burst into laughter. "Fuck. God. You think my parents would be that awful? Hi, I'm Dick. Dick Strong."

"Well, my mother named me Daisy when our last name is Deforest."

I cringe on her behalf, though secretly I think the name is adorable. Daisy Deforest. Come here, Daisy. Daddy needs a goodnight kiss.

Shit.

Shit.

Shit.

"Well, there are worse names. One of the nurses who used to work here was Matthew Bates. Can you guess what his nickname was?"

Her teeth come out to chew her lip as she thinks, and I'm captivated by the sight. I can tell the moment she gets the joke because she gives a startled little gasp and those eyes, those beautiful big eyes stare up at me, scandalized. "Masturbate?" she whispers, gaze darting around to make sure no one else in the hall can see us. As if that word is still wicked and shocking to her.

Fuck, I hope it is.

Before she can see my dick rising to full mast, I spin around and face the vending machine. I shove my card roughly into the chip reader and punch a code twice in repetition. Two granola bars fall into the collection pan and I retrieve my card and them, subtly putting my hand in my pocket and then tucking my boner into my waistband in the process.

Then I turn and hand one to Daisy. "Breakfast."

Her mouth purses. "Ugh–"

I shake a finger at her, and then, out pops a phrase that sets the tone for everything to come between us. Low and husky, I state, "Daddy knows best."

* * *

5 MONTHS LATER

I SHOULDN'T HAVE DONE it. I shouldn't have gotten involved. Her mother's case wasn't surgical, but the way Daisy's eyes lit up when I offered to review her mother's case clinched it. I had to.

That was just the first meeting of many I had with them, until meetings became hang outs, and hang outs became dinners. Trying to be helpful, but also because I couldn't stay away from that laugh. I'd stop by with flowers, card games— any excuse to try and wrangle a laugh out of Daisy.

Her mother, Darla, was sweet and kind, but it was Daisy who made the room light up. Daisy whose shy smiles and snarky retorts made my stomach skip like rocks across a pond.

I thought about asking her out dozens of times. Hundreds. I'm not shy; I typically consider myself aggressive. But hitting on a woman in a bar is so completely different from hitting on a woman with heartbreak haunting her eyes.

No matter how much we talked and laughed, her worried gaze always slid back to her mother. It never stayed on me. Her face always grew pensive and haunted.

I knew what I had to do—what she needed.

There was an experimental trial I could get her mother into … I had a friend who owed me a favor. But insurance wouldn't cover it, the costs were out-of-pocket.

Daisy and her mother would never have taken a check.

So I came up with another solution. It was probably a terrible idea. I was probably shooting myself in the foot by doing it. But that's when the demon appeared on my shoulder. Because if I did it, Daisy would always be mine. Maybe not the way I wanted, but still … *mine*.

The funny thing about morality is … it's not nice and neat like science. It can't be put into a box. It's more like water in a glass. Once that glass is cracked, all of the water will slowly trickle out.

Mine.

That word started to become an obsession for me.

The trickle began before I even proposed to Darla. The crack widened when she said yes.

On the surface, the marriage ensured Darla could get better insurance and that special treatment, though other people made all the romantic assumptions they wanted about us. But underneath, in this dark little corner of my head that I tried to ignore … it ensured that somehow, some way, Daisy would always be mine.

Even as Daisy walks her mother down the aisle in the hospital chapel—a room set up with empty wooden benches, linoleum, and scented by antiseptic instead of flowers—it's Daisy's long, slim legs I look at, her svelte figure, the column of her neck where her brunette hair is swept up into a pony-tail full of curls.

There is no audience. She and her mother don't speak to extended family. Grandparents gone. Daisy's biological father is a mystery …they didn't have anyone to invite. Daisy's mother is the only family she has in the whole world … and she's about to lose her—which is how I justify every-thing to myself.

But I didn't invite anyone on my side, worried they'd see through me, worried that my depravity would leak out through my expressions, that they'd take one look into my eyes and realize how utterly fucking evil I'd become.

Because it is evil.

But I can't stop myself from doing it.

Flickering rows of red votive candles full of prayers light the wall behind her, but no one realizes that instead of summoning angels, there's a demon in their midst.

Daisy weeps for joy as she walks down the aisle towards me in an innocent tea-length dress of pale yellow, full of the belief that her mother gets some sort of fairytale ending. Sweet, innocent little Daisy has no idea I wanted to be her villain, not her mother's prince.

Stuck in a tux with a bow tie that's cutting off my air flow, my smile at Daisy is genuine. But so is my attraction, which always crops up at the most inconvenient times. My girl takes my breath away as she walks toward me, and I have to cup my hands in front of myself to hide the hard-on I got just from staring at her.

I try to talk myself down. I have to remind myself that she just turned nineteen—is about to have to inhale and swallow a shitstorm of pain—and this is the long game I'm playing. I have to remind myself that Darla's a good person, a good soul, and even if she isn't my soulmate, she created my soulmate and deserves the utmost respect.

I tell that monster in my chest that wants to grab at Daisy's hands instead of her mother's that he has to wait, and I rein him in. Control him. Just like I do with everything else in life.

I speak the vows to be loyal to Darla for the rest of her life, but both she and I know the truth. It's only a matter of time. Treatment isn't working. Even the experimental program I've gotten her into—one where she'd be so pumped full of radiation that we wouldn't be able to be in the same room with her for a week at a time—won't do much but delay the inevitable.

I'm buying her time, not a cure.

But time is a gift Daisy needs.

I take Darla's hands in mine and speak halting vows in a gruff tone after the chaplain. But on the line, "I will be yours for all the days of my life," I glance over at Daisy instead of her mother. Because I speak those words to her.

GUNNAR

12 MONTHS LATER

"*D*aisy, hurry up! You're going to be late!" I call up the stairs as morning light filters in through the arched front hall windows. My voice echoes off the tiled floor but soaks into the adobe accent wall, the mud bricks swallowing the sound. I sigh as the grandfather clock in the corner ticks on, the pendulum a little squeaky because I need to get it serviced. It's close to eight, and if she doesn't get a move on, my sweet Daisy is going to miss her first class.

There's no response from above.

Dammit.

I've been trying to give her space and let her mourn. Trying not to let loose the animal inside my brain trying to tell me it's finally time. The one who makes me stand outside her door at night, listening to her even breathing after she's cried herself to sleep. The one who makes me go inside and stare at her. I won't give in to him. Not yet. I know I won't be able to hold him back forever … but she's not ready yet.

I'm going to have to be patient. She's still healing.

I start up the stairs, wondering what the hell I'm going to be up against this morning. The first two weeks after her mother passed, Daisy was practically comatose. Understandable. The two months after that, she would get out of bed to shower and eat and then slide right back under the covers. The past two months, I've coaxed her into getting up long enough to go volunteer at an animal shelter for a couple hours a day. I've been taking care of her: cooking for her, teaching her to cook, helping her do chores when she's too melancholy to get up.

But after four and a half months of mourning, I have to do something. She can't stay holed up in her room forever—she'll never move forward that way.

Darla was a good woman. I might not have loved her, but I respected her. Even at the end, the woman had grit—sarcasm and banter pouring from her mouth during her final days. And I know exactly what she'd want for her daughter. She'd want Daisy to go on living. Find happiness. And happiness isn't lurking behind her bedroom door. I am. I'm not going to be a lurker much longer though.

The second semester just started and my girl is finally going to start college.

I push open the second door on the right, the door to Daisy's bedroom. Her room is nothing like the rest of the house, which has typical Southwestern decor. I had it decorated for her when they first moved in, and her choices had surprised me. Daisy had wanted everything shabby chic, light-blue walls, a hand knotted rug, a quilt, and that old furniture that's repainted white to look worn.

She hadn't wanted a TV, telling me that watching it before going to sleep was bad for you, with a pointed look that said she disapproved of the sixty-inch monstrosity on my own bedroom wall.

In addition to the typical teenage collection of band posters and twenty pounds of unnecessary makeup, she also had a collection of teddy bears.

I'd scoffed when I helped her unpack them all those months ago.

"Aren't you a little old for these, Daise?" I'd asked, pulling one of a dozen bears out of a box. It was a small white bear in a black vest, hardly as big as my palm.

"Excuse me," she'd grabbed her precious stuffed animal out of my hands and hugged it defensively to her chest. "But do you even know the origin of the teddy bear?"

"No."

"It was named after Teddy Roosevelt because he refused to shoot a bear on a hunting trip."

"Okay…" I'd tried to follow her logic and not the way the bear drew my attention to her breasts.

She'd turned away, and I still remember how her white sundress had swirled around her legs as she marched over and set the little white fur ball on her bookshelf as she continued, "Someone else caught the bear and tied it up for him to shoot. But he said it was unsportsmanlike."

I'd dug another stuffie out of her box, this one a bit smaller and stiffer than the last. "And?"

She'd snorted derisively at me, hurrying over to snatch the new bear away. Her eyes had shone bright blue that afternoon, even as her nostrils flared in annoyance. "It's because life isn't supposed to be *easy*."

It had been a profound moment for me, one that had set me back on my heels where I knelt in front of her. She was so young … but my Daisy was deeper than the Mariana Trench. Pride was an emotion I'd been familiar with on my own—some assholes at work said I was too familiar with it, typical surgeon-slandering B.S. But that day, I'd realized just how intense pride in someone else can be. My chest had warmed and expanded and the smile that crossed my face was soft and awed.

She'd plucked at the tan fur of the little bear in her hands. "I got this bear when my soccer team lost when I was six years old. My mom refused to let me have the participation trophy." She had chuckled at the memory.

"Sounds like Darla," I'd agreed, smiling up at her, drinking in the way laughter made her cheeks grow pink. "This one?" I'd pulled out a new bear.

She grimaced and came forward to take it into her arms next to the other. "When Christian Rockford—my sixth-grade crush—made fun of me."

"That little shit," I'd stood, playfully kicking her box of bears dramatically to the side. "Tell me where he lives now, and I'll go beat him up for you." I gorilla-thumped my chest.

"Oh god." She'd rolled her eyes and laughed, but by her expression, I could tell she liked my caveman act. "Calm down, Gunnar."

I'd frozen, startled by the effect hearing my name had on me. It was strange. She'd said my name countless times over the months … but somehow, having her say it here in my house … laughing, smiling that smile I loved—it made everything I'd done to that point feel right.

"Come on, Daise! It's time!" I march through Daisy's room, ignoring the piles of clothes strewn across the wood floor as I stride over to her window and pull apart the curtains. I let the sunshine stream in and disinfect the sadness permeating the very air. "Rise and shine!"

"Go away."

"Nope. You have class today. And if you're going to be a surgeon like me then you need to get up and get going. College waits for no one."

"I quit." She glares petulantly up at me.

"I'm not letting you quit." I cross my arms, showing her I'm serious.

"You can't make me." Her retort is muffled by the covers she pulls back over her head, the quilt patterned with different flowers warping as it molds around her skull.

That will not do. I head to the foot of her bed and grab the edge of the quilt, the blanket underneath, and the sheet. In one fell swoop, I yank them all down. "Wanna bet?"

"Fucker!" Daisy screeches, curling up into a ball against the onslaught of cool, air-conditioned air.

I have to take a moment to remember to breathe when I realize she's only wearing a green t-shirt and some black panties. My entire body overheats, and my pulse thuds automatically, eyes glued to the hem of those conservative little bikini briefs.

Not yet.

She's not ready.

Not yet.

I groan internally, because I've already been waiting so fucking long. But I glance over at Daisy's teddy bears and remind myself that life isn't supposed to be easy. My sweet little Daisy isn't easy. And it's going to be better because she's not.

I hope I can convince her that I'm not just some guy who married her mom. Not just her stepdad.

I want to be her daddy.

Ever since the first moment we met at that vending machine, it's all I can think about.

God, I'm so fucked up. Who does what I've done? Who meets a barely-legal girl and then sets out to infiltrate her life? I've justified it eighty different ways—not wanting her to be alone, needing to take care of her and be her emotional support system ... but underlying all of that is this sick twisted drive to keep her for myself.

A wave of self-loathing rolls through me, but in comparison to my longing for Daisy, it's just a shadow. Just a blot of darkness in my vision, an inconvenience I've learned to live with and work around.

Because no matter how fucked up I am, there's no turning back.

All those thoughts make my voice come out gruffer than it should. "Get up, lazy Daisy. You're twenty. I shouldn't even have to be in here."

"I don't wanna go!" Her bratty side comes out—it used to come out quite often when we first met. But as Darla got worse, it disappeared for a while. Now … it looks like it's back.

If she's ready to play, then so am I.

I narrow my eyes at her. "You are going to get in trouble."

"Oh yeah, what are you going to do, spank me?" she taunts. "Try it! I dare you." Her eyes glare up at me, a mischievous sparkle lighting them up.

My fingers twitch. I don't think she has any idea how much I'd like to do just that.

But her head pops up from the pillow. She turns to stare at me with a look that she thinks is fierce but I can only label adorable. Her brown hair is a messy frizz around her head. One cheek has a bright pink mark from how she slept with her hand tucked underneath it. She licks her lips to wet them and though I hold her gaze to challenge her, I have to internally challenge myself not to imagine what it would look like if I shoved a finger into her mouth and commanded her to suck.

"Give it up, Gunnar. I'm going to live in this bed forever and there's nothing you can do about it."

"I could get rid of the bed," I tell her.

"Then I'll live in the closet like a gremlin."

"I'd say you're too cute to be a gremlin, but actually, this could explain your aversion to showers."

That earns me a pillow to the face. I catch it as it falls, grinning.

"I take showers!" she grumbles.

"Prove it. Go take one."

"I don't need to prove anything to you."

"Get out of bed."

"No."

"Out or I'm going to have to tickle you out of there."

"You wouldn't!" she mockingly gasps but she's biting down on a smile.

I give her a grave look. "Desperate times ..."

She clamps her hands defiantly down on the fitted sheet. Apparently, she's down to play.

Fuck yes. I swallow my smile of triumph—I'm going to get to tickle her—and pour on the commanding vibes as I march around the foot of her bed.

When I reach for her, she quickly rolls to the opposite side and curls up into a ball facing me. I wait a few seconds but she makes no move to get out of the bed. That makes her fair game. I plant a knee on her mattress, knowing my khakis are going to get wrinkled and I'll have to change for the department meeting later. But screw it. I can't pass up a chance to touch her. Tease her. Test the line.

The monster inside my chest roars and rattles his cage.

"Daisy," I balance my weight on one hand and let the other hover over her, fingers wiggling in the most menacing manner that fingers can wiggle. "If you don't get up, I'm going to make you scream. You're going to regret every second."

"Am I?" She grins, and I can see her breathing growing shallow.

Is she … is she into this?

She can't be.

Wishful thinking.

But then she licks her lips and her eyes fall down to my mouth.

Oh, fuck me. I'm screwed.

I let my hand slowly descend like one of those claw games in an arcade.

Daisy's fingers tighten on the fitted sheet and she tenses up her legs. Her movement rucks her shirt up, exposing a tiny sliver of her black panties where they disappear between her thighs.

Goddamn.

I want to take a photograph of this moment. I try to burn into my brain the way it feels to perch on top of Daisy's crisp white fitted sheet as she lets out a string of unladylike curses and I *tsk* at her.

"Do you want to be humiliated screaming for mercy *and* fill up the swear jar in a single morning? You'll be footing my coffee bill for a long time if you keep it up."

"I'm not a fucking child!"

"Of course you aren't. Swearing has nothing to do with that."

"Then what the fuck is the point?"

"Control," I mutter, as much for myself as to answer her question. "Self-control."

"You can't control me." Her voice pitches low and, I want to believe, sultry.

Oh, how much I'm going to enjoy proving her wrong. My hand descends all the way to her middle, cutting off any other argument. My fingers dig in right under her ribs and I relish the way she squirms, accidentally moving closer when she kicks out and screeches. God, she's fucking adorable.

I try to ignore the way her shirt bunches and keep my eyes trained on her face. On how she's actually laughing and the darkness that's been in her eyes for months, since we knew that the end was approaching, has retreated momentarily.

Her little giggles and snorts and the growls as she latches onto my forearm and tries to yank it away from her torso are the real thing. And God, does it make me feel good to see that.

Because as much as I want to fuck her, I also just want to make her happy.

My sentimentality is my downfall because Daisy effectively yanks my hand aside and I go toppling down on top of her. My torso smashes against hers and I hear a huff of breath on impact.

I scramble to get her hands off my arm so that I can lift myself up. I don't want to crush her, the girl's only half my size. But she takes every one of my motions as an attempt at fighting. She locks down harder on my arm and even raises a leg, trying to dig her knee into my side. And suddenly the knee digging into my side is shifting … becoming a calf wrapped around my back.

Holy shit.

This position. I try to look at her face, but her upper half is still fighting me, even as her legs start to clamp suggestively around me.

She can't mean it. It's just a coincidence.

I double down on attacking her with my fingers, which means I give up propping myself up with one hand and just let myself sink on top of her so I can use the hand that was holding myself as my new weapon. I plunder her underarm, wiggling my fingers, noting how my palm skates so deliciously close to the side of her breast.

"Gah! No!" She writhes underneath me and the deviant part of my brain, the broken portion, rearranges her movements inside my head. It becomes dirty.

When her hands come up and her nails rake down my back … it becomes downright obscene.

God, I have to stop this. Right? I have to. We can't just … devolve like this. No. I have plans. Dates. We have to have a discussion … my needs are very … distinct. She might not even want to handle them, but I think … I think she will. I saw something in her bratty eyes the moment we met. Something that makes me believe she'd love all the kinky things I want to do to her.

When she lets go of one of my arms to reach for the other, I see an opening. I snatch both her wrists and pin her hands above her head. Originally, I just meant to hold her still long enough to climb off of her. But we end up staring at one another, her out of breath, me hardly breathing. Because this is exactly how I'd want to hold her the first time I fuck—

No. Nope. I raise my leg and try to move, but her hand snakes out of my grasp like she's an expert criminal slipping out of cuffs. She moves fast and gets my side, trying to tickle me back. I have to counter her attack with a quick swivel of my fingers over her ribs. I hit a spot that makes her howl.

I watch her toss her head side to side as the demon inside me whispers, *That's exactly what she'd be doing if I was fucking her hard and deep right now.*

"OKAY! OKAY! I give!" she pants. "Uncle! Uncle!"

I give her a victory smirk, the thrill of winning and of her surrender coursing through me as I carefully pull my hand away from her ribcage, pushing myself up. I don't release my hold on her remaining hand, because it's so perfect that I can't bring myself to let go before I absolutely have to. My own breathing is as ragged as hers, but for entirely different reasons. But she's not ready. I need to ease her into this. Still, I can't stop the words, "I'm not uncle."

Pinned beneath my body, with her face flushed, and shirt still rucked up deliciously, she glances down my torso before peering up at me from under her lashes. "That's right. You're Daddy."

All the air leaves the room as we stare at each other, the connection I've been hoping for and dreaming about for so long rising up between us, crashing over us. It raises all the hair on my arms, and fills my chest with something warm and bright. That's the first time she's called me that since our first meeting. God, it does things to me.

Then she blushes and ducks her head, a little embarrassed by her own audacity, and the potent moment is broken.

But the connection … that's still humming.

Daisy and I are going to happen. It's a certainty.

And now, I know, even if she's not quite ready to admit it—my girl wants it just as much as I do.

DAISY

I pant, staring up at the ceiling of my room when Gunnar leaves, my insides whirling like dead leaves caught up in an autumn breeze. *What was that? What just happened?*

I try to ignore the hope that creeps in—because something is clearly wrong with me. To try and make what just happened into anything more than an attempt to cheer me up is the stupidest thing I could do. My heart is already broken. I don't think I can handle any more damage.

Besides, hoping for more is wrong. So wrong. Gunnar loved my mother for fuck's sake. Not loved, loved … but he married her. He cared for her enough to marry her so she could get treatment. That means there's a line ….

What would everyone say? God, I can only imagine the stares.

I shove a hand into my brunette tangles and chastise myself. "Not yours. Not yours." He's my stepfather. Twice my age. He'd never ….

"God, get out of bed already and stop thinking about it," I grumble as I shove up into a seated position. *Stupid idiot. You're making life harder than it needs to be. And it's already hard enough.*

I stare over at my desk, where the last bear my mother ever gave me sits. It's a small bean-stuffed bear that's tie-dyed with a peace sign over its heart. Because she wants me to remember she's finally at peace. Or for me to find peace—something that currently feels impossible. My chest aches like someone took a machine gun to it. Every time I think one wound has healed, I find another.

Walking down the hall, even though her bedroom door is closed (because between her treatments and Gunnar's insane surgical schedule, it made more sense for them to sleep in separate rooms) I can't pass by it without thinking of her.

Everywhere I look in the house, I still see her. Reaching for my keys, I'll spot her key ring. Her favorite blanket is still draped over the recliner in the living room. Even though she isn't here, she's still everywhere.

I stare at the bear next to my computer as my eyes blur, but Gunnar's warning call up the stairs snaps me out of it.

"Daisy! Get up and shower or I'll hose you down myself!"

God, that would be fun. I imagine Gunnar in the backyard grass next to the pool, spraying me down with the hose as I squeal, running away in my bikini. *Would he tackle me?*

No, Daise. Empty threat, I tell myself. *Empty threat. He doesn't mean what you want him to mean. He's not going to walk up here and strip you bare, telling you it's all going to be alright and kiss away all your tears, making you forget about everything by using his mouth to give you orgasm after orgasm. You're a stupid little girl with a crush.*

I shove myself off the mattress and stomp over the miniature mountain of all my bedsheets, which Gunnar dumped unceremoniously across my floor.

In the shower under the hot spray of water, I try to clear my head and get myself ready for the day. I'm nervous though.

I skipped the first semester of college to stay with my mom. She'd spiraled quickly after my high school graduation, and we'd known we didn't have much time left. While I don't regret that choice—I treasure the memories of afternoons spent playing cards or just holding her hand when cards were no longer possible—now, I don't know what to expect from college. All my friends will know what they're doing. Have a routine.

What if I feel like the odd girl out?

I wish I could smoke a joint to relax, but Gunnar is all about that "the body is a temple" mindset. He let Mom have them for her pain but if he ever found me with one, I'm sure he'd go ballistic.

He's got a real bossy streak—always trying to force a jacket on me before I step outside in case it gets cold, always slipping vitamin water hydration powder packets into my purse so I have them if I need them. What's odd is how much I like it. When Mom was sick, I had to do laundry, make chicken nuggets if I wanted something to eat, think of everything she couldn't. But Gunnar just takes care of me. He's always thinking ahead, trying to make sure I have what I need. He makes me feel … safe.

And God, do I love the expression he gets on his face when I chal-lenge him. When I talk back. Fuck. That domineering side is so hot ... no. No. New train of thought. My mind slides to a tangential topic, one I thought of before but have never solved.

I wonder why he never got married before ... he's hot. Even Violet says so, and she's the pickiest of my friends.

Tall, with dark hair he keeps short and crisp on the sides like he's in the military, he's got these huge shoulders that make him look more like some barbarian than a surgeon. His brown eyes are lined with the kind of long, straight lashes most women would kill for. And I love the crinkles that form around them when he smiles. His hair is speckled gray on the sides, but that only seems to add to his appeal. The first time I saw him, I nearly swooned. When he'd bantered back after I teased him, the excited adrenaline rush I'd gotten—to this day all I have to do is recall that meeting and I end up with a dreamy smile on my face.

How is Gunnar so perfect?

He's just ... so intimidating and in control. He has it together when I always feel like I'm one step away from falling apart. Maybe that's part of the attraction—the fantasy. I want him to swoop in and save me from myself. Wrap those massive arms around me and just pull me back from the brink of disaster. Use his hands to move down my body—the way my own right hand is doing now.

I skate my fingers down my belly as I lean back and let the hot water sizzle along my skin—I love taking nearly scalding showers.

God, what would his huge hands feel like? Those fingertips of his are almost twice the size of mine. And his control—I can tell by the way he does everything from folding laundry to cutting his steak—every movement counts. Once he learned my body, and how I like small little circles over my clit … I'm certain he'd get it right every single time. His surgeon's hands are precision instruments, after all.

My index finger slides down to stroke my slit, running up and down along my folds. It's so wrong, picturing him while I do it. But I haven't been able to stop myself for over a year —why would I start now?

My crush on my stepfather is my dirty little secret.

No one knows about it. Not even my best friend, Rose. I almost told her once, but the vortex of guilt sucked me under and I'd gotten too scared. Lately, that vortex's pull has been getting weaker. Obviously, this morning … I nearly crossed a line.

I picture Gunnar's eyes as he hovered over me in my bed, pinning me down. The shadow that crossed over his expression—the darkness—was probably just *concern*. In my head that concern twists into longing. In my head, the moment doesn't end with him climbing off of me.

Instead, he leans down and captures my lips with his.

He'd kiss me slow and soft, tentatively at first, his lips just brushing against mine until I reached up and twined my fingers in his hair–signaling that this was okay, that I wanted this, that I've dreamed of this since the first second I saw him.

He'd get aggressive then, because that's how he is. Gunnar takes charge and dives right into anything he does. He'd have my shirt off and my panties bunched around my thighs within seconds.

Palming a breast with my left hand, I pretend he's touching me. "Feel good, baby?" the Gunnar inside my imagination asks.

"Yes, Daddy," I whimper aloud, my back leaning against the cold tiles, letting the hot water drip closer to my opening, down the trimmed little patch of hair until it slides down my pussy. The steamy shower heats up the glass door, cocooning me inside, hiding my naughty fantasy from the world.

Putting my clit between my index and middle fingers I rub up and down along the line of my labia and a shiver of pleasure courses through me. He would be gentle but thorough, tracing his fingers along every inch of me, then pulling me open to slide his fingers along my inner seam, testing my wetness, spreading it around. He'd use that dark stare of his, alert for every little catch in my breath.

"You like that?" he'd ask in that gruff voice of his.

The heat between my thighs starts to grow and expand, swirling through me like a solar storm. I move from palming my breast to plucking at my nipple, adding little sparks of sensation to the mix. I widen my stance and thrust my hips up so the hot water traces paths right down to where I need it.

As my hand works me into a frenzy, my mind sends me over the edge.

Gunnar would lean down over me in bed and whisper in my ear, "You're mine now, you know that? You're all mine." I bet he'd slide one hand up from my breast and wrap his fingers around my neck. He's probably into breath play. It seems like the kind of uber-controlling move that would be up his alley. I hold my breath as I continue to tweak my nipple and touch myself, climbing, climbing, climbing—

"Daisy! You'd better hurry up!" his actual voice floats up the stairs, dimmed by the closed bathroom door.

I pretend he's talking about something other than breakfast. I pretend he's ordering me to hurry up and come for him so he can fuck me hard and fast, just like he likes. His hips would slam into me, jostling me across the bed just like the guys in my dirty books do, the pages I inhale in order to escape the world.

I move my hand faster, up and down as my head starts to feel like it's floating. Flames lick the inside of my thighs as they start to tremble. My head tilts back against the tile, and I imagine Gunnar sucking on my pulse, reveling in how fast he's making it pump. My jaw goes slack, and my vision blurs, so I shut my eyes as my muscles tense.

I whimper as I get close, turning my head from side to side, pulling harder on my nipple, adding a tiny bite of pain. *Hurry up, Daisy,* I think in the low voice Gunnar uses whenever he insults the hospital administration. *Hurry up and come so I can stretch that pussy with my cock and make you come again.*

Fuck.

I buck against my hand, grinding my palm against my low belly as my fingers fly, and I fall apart.

As I come back down from the high, I pant, leaning my head back against the tile and staring at the spray from the shower. Yeah, my dirty little crush is wrong. But it feels so damn good.

DAISY

I smooth my white cutoff shirt down self-consciously as I hurry downstairs to breakfast. Lily picked this outfit. The short shirt is paired with tight jeans and a loose pink sweater that I absolutely, under no circumstances, am allowed to button closed. She swears it's what everyone's wearing. Honestly, the only thing about this outfit that feels normal is the pair of tennis shoes. But ... first impressions. I need to look good today.

Gunnar's eyes scan me over, his mouth tightening when his gaze lands on that expanse of exposed skin between my ribs and navel. He hates it. But at least he doesn't comment and make my cheeks burn any more than they already are as I pad around the marble counter so I can grab the plate he made up for me. Egg whites with spinach and cheese and half a slice of avocado toast.

"Thanks." My voice comes out breathy, the way it always does when I'm nervous and my throat tightens up. God, what would he think if he knew what I'd just done in the shower? If he knew I was thinking about him? I'm pretty sure my cheeks turn the same color as my sweater. Bright, blazing pink.

I'm not sure what makes me more nervous; the thought of school or the sight of him looking crisp and put together, facing me in a white collared shirt and gray slacks that mold to his body. He's so sophisticated, so put together. Meanwhile, I'm not at all.

"You're going to have a great day." His hand on my shoulder stops me with my fingers on the edge of my plate.

I freeze and turn to look up at him, looking so solemn and certain. "I don't think you've ever been scared of anything in your entire life."

"You'd be surprised." He gives me a flat look as his big palm traces down my arm leaving a tingling, utterly inappropriate awareness in its wake. Dammit. I shouldn't have touched myself to thoughts of him this morning because now my brain is buzzing, naughty thoughts circling me like a cloud of unwanted gnats.

"I just don't know what to expect. The campus is huge, and all these people will already know each other and have friends. I'm already behind …." Worries come spilling out one after another.

Gunnar turns me then, using his arm to gently nudge me until I face the counter instead of him. Both hands slide up my arms until he cups my shoulders, his warmth sinking into me as his fingers dig in, a slow, steady massage. "You're just starting out. The rooms will be giant lecture halls that look kind of like lame sports stadiums cut in half. There will be a screen and a projector and a professor with a huge nose whose voice sounds like a frog mated with a braying donkey—"

He makes me laugh, my shoulders shaking, ruining any of the relaxing effects of the massage. "Why a huge nose?"

"All my professors had weird noses. I think it's a thing."

"It's definitely not a thing."

"Take pictures on your phone today and we'll compare them over dinner. Bet you a hundred bucks all your teachers have sucky noses. I'll DoorDash some Bánh mì."

"You don't have to. I can cook," I offer, even though Bánh mì is my absolute favorite and Gunnar knows it.

"It's your reward for being brave today." His hands slide away from my shoulders and down my arms, wrapping around my waist as he pulls me back against him in a hug. My head settles back against his chest and I soak in the feeling of being comforted, cared for, reassured. I loved my mother, but cancer is a beast that steals away a parent's ability to give you those things. I lived in uncertainty for so long, it felt like I was tiptoeing on glass.

Gunnar squeezes me harder, and my ass ends up pressed against him. Fuck. Either he's naturally a shower, or he's hard right now.

Get your mind out of the gutter, Daisy. You're ruining a nice moment.

I feel even more guilty when Gunnar places a soft, innocent kiss on the top of my head.

See? Idiot. He's just comforting you.

I force myself to tune back into the conversation, because Gunnar sometimes ends up on a soap box when he's trying to encourage me. "You'll see. Today is just new and different. But those things don't have to be scary. In fact, they can be a good thing." His fingertips lightly graze the bare skin of my stomach in a move I'm certain is purely accidental.

I wish it wasn't.

I reach up to place my hands on top of his. "I know. I know it can be a good thing."

We stay like that for a minute, him engulfing me in this hug as I selfishly soak it in. He's so good and solid, and has been there for me even on the worst days, most of which he's seen.

But then his fingers sweep deliberately back and forth across my belly, his pinkie fingers dragging over the very tops of my hip bones where they emerge from my jeans.

Heat flares across my skin just from his simple touch and I catch my breath. Twice in one day, he's touching me. Twice in one morning. I don't want him to stop. Lava drips down my spine and bubbles in my belly. God, he's hardly grazing my skin but I'm suddenly burning hot.

"Do you really think this is what you should be wearing to school?" His tone is light, just like his touch, but his meaning is clear.

My throat dries out. "Lily said—"

"I didn't ask what Lily said. I'm not Lily's daddy. I'm yours."

I'm yours. Ugh, I wish he was mine. And he had to use that word. Daddy. Something about that word ... how dirty and forbidden it is .... I have to resist the urge to press my thighs together as heat flares through me.

"Look. I'm not—" I start to defend the outfit but he interrupts.

"Daisy, I'm trying to control myself here. But you are making that *really* impossible."

I freeze up at the darkness that creeps into his tone. *Shit. Is he actually pissed about this outfit? But if so, why are his fingers making soft little circles on my skin?*

He continues, "I don't think this is the sort of thing a young lady wears to class when she plans on studying her subjects. This looks like an outfit for a girl interested in studying boys instead."

I can't believe we're having this conversation. Gunnar's always been strict about being on time, keeping the house clean, and curfew. But he's never commented on my clothes before. Of course, I've never let Lily dress me up either and I'm more conservative than she is. I'm torn between mortification and this strange, perverse little instinct telling me there's an undertone of jealousy in his words.

I'd know for sure if I rubbed my ass back and forth against his hips ... if his dick twitched against me. But I'm not brave enough for that. Not brave enough to test him when he's already snapping like a crocodile.

My words come out weak as I search for some way to smooth things over. "I don't—"

"Am I paying for you to go study *boys*?" Gunnar's tone takes on the sharp edge, snapping like a whip, making me cringe.

My face is burning, my pulse thumping loudly in my ears as shame crawls up and makes every inch of me from the neck up turn bright pink. "No."

He grunts, his fingers digging into me for just a second before he releases me. "Then go change."

I immediately scramble forward to do what he asks.

The smack on my ass is unexpected—it stings and makes me gasp in shock. But as I hurry up the stairs, the sting fades to a prickle that morphs into a longing throb.

I imagine him spanking me for real … fuck. Now it's not just my shirt I need to change. My panties have to go too.

* * *

"I DIDN'T THINK math could be more boring. But add a Russian accent that makes it unintelligible and boom! I couldn't even pretend to concentrate." Rose rolls her dark brown eyes as she sets down her tray at one of the outdoor picnic tables surrounding the Student Union building. The big, ugly block structure behind us is a cesspit full of shallow chit-chat and diabetes-inducing scents. It's way too crowded for me. I'm used to quiet hospital hallways and lots of time at the house. But I slap on a smile because this is going to be my new normal. And it will be fine.

Though there are plenty of tables in the shade, and some open near the grassy knolls surrounding the campus duck pond, Rosie picks one in the sun, because she's a Vitamin D addict. Give that girl sunshine and a dirty book and she's set for hours.

She's lucky the weather is cooperating with her preferences today. Even though it's mid-January, Albuquerque is going through a strange wave of decent weather. The wind is non-existent and it's sixty degrees, though it feels warmer when the sun soaks into your shoulders for a bit, which I'm certain is Rose's plan. The other Wild Flowers and I follow her to a square table.

Only elementary school girls could think that having floral names was a solid reason for starting up a lifelong friendship. But stranger things have happened. Our little foursome has been together since we were seven years old.

We've seen each other through Rose's parents' divorce, Violet's discovery that her family is a little, tiny bit tied to the Irish mob (as in majorly tied—hogtied), and of course, my mom's—I can't even think the word.

Other than Gunnar, these girls are my family. My loud, chatty, *opinionated* family.

"I thought the T.A. was hot," Lily disagrees, flipping her long auburn hair over her shoulder. She's the loudest and most beautiful of the group. She even had a stalker in high school, some guy who traced her social media and showed up at her door. She had to get a restraining order and everything, and he eventually got sent to jail—which made her a bit of a high school celebrity.

"You think everyone's hot." Violet sets a dish of cold handmade pasta salad on the table next to me as she slings her backpack over the back of the seat. Conservative, an excellent cook who taught me everything I know, and completely fluent in both Spanish and Italian—Violet looks like a girl who has her life all put together. But the four of us know things aren't always what they seem. Violet actually has zero control over her own destiny. In a way, that makes me sad. But, in another way, I long for the comfort of knowing what's coming next, of my family solving my problems for me, someone else taking care of me. She's lucky, and she doesn't know it.

"Did anyone think that T.A. had a weird nose?" I ask as I sit.

"Could you even see his nose? He was looking at the board most of the time," Rose comments as she digs into some chicken nuggets she snagged inside. She pushes a black curl behind her ear, revealing a gold heart-shaped earring as she dips a nugget into sauce.

Gunnar would get so pissed if I was eating that. I sit down across from Rose and set my backpack on my lap and unzip it to find the lunch he packed me. I used to resist him on this stuff. Takeout was all I had in high school when Mom was sick. But somewhere along the way ... it just got easier to submit. And then ... one day, I started to like eating healthy and then even cooking healthy.

I yank out an icepack and dig underneath it to find a fresh fruit salad, crackers, and tuna fish sandwich ... she out to sabotage me? Seriously? He's giving me tuna breath on day one?

I purse my lips and consider texting him something snarky. But he had a surgery scheduled for midday, so he won't even have his phone on him. Jerk.

I can hear all his arguments about omega-threes inside my head but part of me wonders—the same part of me that wondered about changing clothes this morning—if something else is going on.

His behavior is weird. But it's also weirdly possessive. Why is it that the former is a big fat nope from me, but the latter ...? Well, I wouldn't mind the latter. If Gunnar wants me to change out of hot clothes and give me wildly bad breath to keep college guys away because he wants me for himself—

But what if I'm just making things up? Overthinking? I mean, other than Mom's live-in nurses and my girls here, I haven't seen anyone but the other animal shelter volunteers in months. My humaning is not necessarily on point right now and my imagination might be a little too fine-tuned.

The only person I could possibly ask about all of this is Rose —because we're closest, but also because I know she has a crush on someone who would piss her brother off.

But there's zero chance I'll get her alone before her English class in half an hour. Not when Lily and I have World History in forty-five minutes. Shit.

I bite down on my lip as I stare at a couple of students carrying tennis rackets walking across campus. How am I supposed to decide if I'm pissed about this sandwich situation or thrilled? If Gunnar is trying to sabotage my chances with guys on campus, does it even mean he's interested? Or is it just another aspect of his overprotective, controlling nature?

If he's interested … which is a fucking long shot … what does that even mean? What about Mom? Is it a betrayal? Is it bad?

Rose has told me repeatedly that we can't help who we're drawn to—it's written in the stars. She likes to be all die-hard romantic about it.

But if it was written in the stars, why did he marry my mother?

I reach over and steal one of Rose's nuggies, ignoring the way her big brown eyes widen at the theft as she swats at my hand. I need some diabetes-inducing caloric relief for all the heavy mental processing I'm doing here.

"I've already taken Algebra I in high school, so at least the class is easy," Lily continues the conversation from where she sits catty-corner to me. Her auburn hair is up in a French twist, her nails are perfectly manicured, and she's eyeing my pink tank top skeptically. "What happened to that shirt I bought you?"

"Spilled coffee on it," I lie, making an apologetic face.

Immediately, she rolls her eyes because it is totally something I would do. "Knew I should have gotten it in black instead of white."

I have to swallow a sigh of relief as the topic goes back to the T.A. who just led our math class with his back to the room—facing the board the entire time as he muttered completely unintelligible shit. Higher education. What a joke.

That guy won't be teaching us a thing. And math isn't what I really need to learn anyway. I need to learn how to read a guy's face and tell if he's into me or not. Or—in the very likely scenario that he's not—I need to learn how to turn off my idiotic heart and—

My thoughts trail off as a random guy strides right up to us. He's lanky, with curly black hair that's shorn on the sides and a cute disaster on top. He's wearing a funny science shirt with an image of an atom and the phrase "You Matter." I chuckle under my breath.

He stops at our table, right in between Rose and me. "Hey. I'm in Algebra with you. I'm Justin." To my surprise, he doesn't look at everyone else. Just at me.

"Oh. Hey." I give him an awkward smile-nod combination, wondering what the hell is going on. When we're in a group, it's *always* Lily who gets the attention. Not me. I'm the shy one. At least until I get to know you. Then I'm a font of sarcasm.

"Um …" He swipes awkwardly at his neck. "You probably don't remember me, but we were at the Ronald McDonald house at the same time for a while. I was there for my brother. Remember?"

It would hurt less if he'd taken a bulldozer and scooped out the front half of my body. That was the worst of times. It was before Gunnar—when social workers had been coming to talk to me about where I might end up if I was a minor when Mom passed because treatment wasn't going well.

I have absolutely zero recollection of this guy whatsoever. I've blanked out and erased those months and then scribbled over them in permanent marker. "Oh. Yeah." My voice comes out thin and reedy.

"Anyway. It's good to see you somewhere else," he gives a shaky laugh that I don't know how to interpret. "If you want to study together sometime, let me know."

"Ok, sure." I'm nodding and smiling, just hoping he'll go away and let me get rid of the miserable slideshow that's currently playing behind my eyes—other memories besides the house that I haven't been able to block. Sad doctor's faces. Test results. Before Gunnar got Mom into that experimental treatment, things had looked so bleak.

He swooped in like a guardian angel and gave us hope for a bit. And then … when all was hopeless, he was still there. Letting us cry on his shoulder. Forcing both of us to eat. Requiring family movie night ….

Fuck. If I don't stop, I'm going to cry. I blink and smile harder up at the stranger.

"Great!" This guy is about as great at reading the room as I am. "How about Thursday night?"

"Sure. Yeah."

"Library? Or we can go to my dorm if—"

"Library's good. Great." I try to signal Rose with my eyes, sending out an S.O.S. But my Latina friend simply blinks in amusement. Meanwhile, my palms are sweating and I'm not certain but I think my toenails might have dug holes right through the soles of my shoes because even my feet are tensed up and cringing. This is a disaster.

"Eight okay? Third floor?"

What is happening right now?

"Yup. Great. Good. See you then." Social niceties spew from my mouth on autopilot, just like they did at Mom's funeral. I want to gouge out my own eyes as he gives me a crooked smile.

"Awesome. Can I just get your number so I can text you?"

No.

But Justin whips out his phone and I don't know how to refuse. I type in my number, trying not to let my fingers shake. Meanwhile, across the table, Lily is slurping her soda through a straw and her eyes are ping-ponging back and forth between us like this is a fucking TV show.

Finally, he leaves and I can exhale. Breathe normally. Glance around at the faces at the table. "Traitors! What the hell was that?"

Violet gives a shrug. "What was what?"

Some kind of spazzy, cartoonish pointing in the direction of Justin's back happens—I'm not really in control of myself right now. I'm freaking out.

"Calm down, Daisy. It's just a date."

"Just a date! Just a date!" Easy for her to say. She's been dating since she was sixteen. I was sixteen when Mom first got diagnosed. Then we moved for treatment for a bit, before it didn't seem to matter, and we moved back. And then ... well, I've had other priorities.

"Look, maybe it will be a good thing," Rose's tone is cautious. "You know, get the first one out of the way with a guy you don't really like ... that way you aren't nervous when a guy you're really interested asks."

A little bit of panic breathing sets in, and I don't know if I want to laugh or throw my fruit salad in her lap. "Are you fucking kidding me?"

"It's what I did," Lily's tone is so matter-of-fact. "You should probably just get the kissing thing out of the way with him though. Practice that since you're rusty. I'd say sex ... but let's be real, he doesn't look like he knows how to show a girl a good time."

"True," the other girls chorus.

I grab my fork and stab a cube of honeydew, shoving it into my mouth. I'm certain that if I were to speak right now, I'd end up screaming.

The Wild Flowers are just calmly discussing the merits of me giving away my virginity to cancer-house dude like it's no big deal.

I kick Rose under the table. She jolts, hissing in pain, and giving me an annoyed look, but I think I finally get through to her when I forcefully stab a piece of cantaloupe.

She holds up her hands and stops the group chatter. "Okay, okay, enough. You can no-show the date, alright, Daise? Just text him and say you aren't feeling good."

"I love to say I'm on my period." Violet offers a suggestion that is absolutely, one hundred percent not something I'd ever say to some guy I've just met. Of course, she takes drastic measures to ward off guys her family doesn't approve of.

"Just say you came down with something. You don't have to tell him what." Rose's approach is gentler.

"You need to go," Lily's voice brooks no argument. "You need to go so that you can get over this obsession you have with Doctor Strong."

All the color leaves my face. She knows?

I glance at Rose who gives me a subtle shrug. Do they all fucking know?! I want to melt and sink into a crack in the concrete right now—how fucking embarrassing!

"Come on. It's obvious." Lily folds her arms on the table and leans forward, her lips enunciating every word of my night-mare. "But he's your step dad, Daisy. Hot as fuck. But you have to realize it's never going to happen. And wishing it was is just going to leave you miserable." Her hand reaches across the table, gentle as she touches mine. Her voice softens to match her touch. "I just want you to be happy, Daise."

Happy.

It's been so long since I've been fully happy, I'm not even sure what that would look like. I've been fantasizing it would be with Gunnar … but maybe that's all it is. A fantasy.

GUNNAR

"*L*ook at his nose. That's a total scimitar. I bet he could slash through your test papers with that thing. Looks sharp as fuck." I glare playfully at the T.A. in the photo on Daisy's phone. "I'm right. They all have terrible noses."

"You are ridiculous. The tip is a little sharp, I'll give you that. But there's the tiniest little curve there!" Daisy leans sideways on the soft gray sectional where we sit side by side. My food is already finished, carton set beside me. Hers is only half-done, the takeout container perched precariously on her crossed legs, legs that are deliciously bare because she changed into a baby blue pajama set before dinner.

Fuck, I love the sight of her skin.

I try not to turn into her as she presses a breast against one of my shoulders, her body soft against me as she peers at her phone—which I'm currently holding so I can flick through the pics she took today of unsuspecting professors. In front of us, a fire crackles in the two-story kiva fireplace, giving

49

more ambiance than actual warmth—but I love the scent of the piñon wood and the cozy little picture we make. I'm in a great mood—Surgery went smoothly today, a solid ten followed by some easy meetings, and Daisy enjoyed her first day at the University of New Mexico, and now I'm thoroughly enjoying teasing her.

"It's a terrible nose. Tell me you can see it's a terrible nose." I glance over at her. "If you can't, maybe we need to get your eyes checked."

"I think you're nose-ist!"

I swallow a chuckle as I jab a finger at the guy's nose, which could give a toucan a run for its money. "I am not! That's *not* a tiny curve. It's massive!"

"It's like a little bitty hump."

"That's a Nascar-level turn there. It's huge."

"Guys always overestimate size."

My eyebrows shoot up as I glance over at the blush I can see creeping up her cheeks. My eyes twinkle as I ask, "Oh, do we?"

"Yes." She's adorably embarrassed but won't back down. She adopts a superior attitude, pursing her lips. God, she's fucking cute.

"Please, go on."

"You know what I mean."

There's no way I'm letting her off the hook that easily. "I don't think I do. What do we overestimate?"

Our gazes clash and warmth zings down my belly but it's not just sexual. I absolutely adore teasing my Daisy this way. She's always so snappy and unpredictable.

"Fish."

Her answer surprises me so much that a laugh bursts out. Clever little thing

She capitalizes on her win, expanding on her answer for both of our amusement. "You know, when you catch those tiny little wiggly things and then pretend they're monsters?" Her fingers pinch together and expand as wide as her little hands can stretch. A naughty playfulness lights her up and I wish I could capture it and bottle it, so I could drink in that expression over and over again. "You make tiny little tadpoles into foot-long piranhas!"

"Piranhas! I don't think piranhas are a foot long!"

"Exactly!" She shoves playfully at me.

"But what if they are? What if you're wrong?" I pause and let my face become exaggeratedly serious. "It's time for a Google off!"

Daisy play-gasps, clapping her hands to her cheeks, pretending to be scared, though her mouth quickly curves up in delight.

Google off is a game we like to play where we test one another's statements. The rules are this—we have to name the stakes. Then we google the answer to our debated issue. The first result is accepted as our absolute truth. The loser has to suffer the consequences.

Daisy closes her takeout container and sets it behind her before crossing her arms and narrowing her eyes. In a tone that would rival any cowboy in a Western shoot-out movie, she says, "Name your terms."

"If piranhas are over a foot long then I get … a foot massage." I laugh at my own cleverness but honestly, my pick is no surprise. It's my favorite consequence, though there are a few fantasy consequences that flit through my mind. My favorite one is Daisy on her knees, her hair gathered up into a pony-tail by one of my hands as her plush lips fall open and her warm, wet mouth engulfs the head of my cock.

"Ugh, that was such a bad dad joke. And I knew you'd pick that!" She gives my arm a weak, playful slap accompanied by a long-suffering expression.

"Ouch! Assault!" I rub at my arm.

She laughs. "You poor baby! Here." She leans forward and plants a gentle kiss on my arm, one I can hardly feel through my shirt, but it nonetheless sends sparks writhing through me. I stop breathing as she sits back up.

I notice her pupils are blown out and her breathing is shal-low. Could it mean what I want it to mean? I study every inch of her face, wondering, as she opens her mouth and names her terms. "I want a back massage. A real one. Not two seconds on my shoulders and done."

Fucking hell. I hope I lose. May the Google gods be against me.

There is nothing I want more on this Earth than to slide my fingers over every inch of her exposed skin, unless it was to slide my tongue over it instead. Maybe I could convince her that I need to take her shirt off to massage her properly. I picture sliding my fingers underneath her bra straps, pretending they get in the way too, gently moving them aside.

She's never picked this consequence before. God ... today is changing everything. And I'm here for it.

The way her gaze is flickering across mine, the way I realize I can see the shape of her nipples growing taut, pressing up underneath her shirt ... there is no bra to shove aside. She's definitely not wearing one. My fantasy morphs so that she's sprawled on the gray carpet in front of the fireplace shirtless, the sides of her small breasts visible as I rub up and down her spine, straddling her. Maybe my fingers will slip, caressing the edges of those soft globes. Maybe I can make it feel so good she ends up moaning.

I end up squeezing her phone harder than I intend—I'm so fucking turned on.

This might be so much easier than I ever imagined. But in the year and a half or so that I've known her, I've imagined so many things. The kink that popped up from the moment I met her has only grown. I love this girl ... but I also want to do very bad things to her.

Is that the sort of thing she can accept?

Or will I scare her off?

The temptress smile and sultry eyes she's giving me makes the darkness in me rise, filling my chest and my mind like smoke. It takes everything I have not to just grab her and shove her back on the couch so I can teach her what Daddy likes, the way I've imagined doing hundreds of times.

No.

Every last bit of my self-control wrestles down that salivating monster, the beast panting inside me. I can't scare her like that. I'll lose her.

Unaware of the battle inside of me, of the danger she's in, Daisy morphs out of sexual goddess mode and motorboats her lips the way she always does when she's impatient. She adds a finger snap as she commands, "Hurry! Let's see!" She leans forward, reaching for her phone, but I hold it aside, out of her grip, making her stretch until she's so damn close to falling over in my lap.

One little push and she'd be splayed across my legs.

God.

I turn away slightly. "I've got it." I swipe and unlock her phone, ignoring her startled exclamation about the fact that I know her password. I don't just know this password. I know her computer password. I know her social media passwords.

A good daddy checks on his gir—SHUT UP! I shout at my brain, which is quickly going off the rails, right when I need to be the most careful. I'm so close to getting what I want. So close. I can't let this obsession trip me up.

Typing into Google, I search "biggest piranha" and hit enter. Then I hold the screen up so we can both easily see the results. The little card that pops up on the top of the screen states:

San Francisco Piranha

Native to Brazil, the San Francisco Piranha can grow up to thirteen inches and weigh up to seven pounds.

Goddammit.

"Booo!" Daisy's playful pout is so much happier than the fit that's occurring inside my head. I'm fucking livid that I won. Normally a competitive dick, a stereotypical surgeon who can't stand to lose, this moment is turning everything on its head—because the fucking foot massage is a shit prize compared to what I almost got to have.

Fucking internet. Stupid game.

But Daisy bounds up off the couch and kneels on the floor, reaching for my left shoe.

"You don't have to—"

She gives me a sultry look that hits me so hard I have to lean back in my seat. "Yes I do." She finishes unlacing my black shoe and tugs it off. "Those are the rules. I have to follow the rules."

Hell yes, you do.

I shut up because her tone of voice, her use of *that* word, the one we use when we're playing—bantering—testing that line tells me I need to give in. Combined with the sight of her on the ground in front of me, it's a triple threat that's completely irresistible.

I let her tug off my sock and then bare my other foot. Her tiny little fingers clutch both of my feet for a moment, and though I don't have anything close to a foot fetish, for a second, I imagine commanding her to suck on my toes … just to see if she would.

Would she give in to me? Would she let me dominate her the way I've always wanted to?

She sets my right foot down and then moves both hands over to my left foot, positioning her thumbs in my arch the way I like. I'm leaning back against the couch, preparing to close my eyes and try to enjoy this in a nonsexual way—if that's even possible with her—when her phone vibrates in my palm.

Automatically, I swipe up and put in her passcode to open it, even as she dives across my body to grab it.

"Hey! That's mine!"

"One of the Wild Flowers having a crisis?" I tease, because she doesn't typically get evening texts unless it's from them.

But the text message makes me freeze. Because the very first line says …

Hey, Daisy, it's Justin.

A guy? A guy is texting her! My blood starts to boil and I push Daisy's hand away more roughly than I intend to so that my eyes can scan the remainder of the text.

I just wanted to confirm our study date plans for Thursday. And check in to see if the rest of your day was good.

A date.

The beast I've been wrangling roars, grabbing the bars of his mental cage and wrenching them aside with a horrible screech as I stand up, causing Daisy to fall back to the floor with a distressed little cry. Rage overtakes me and I throw the phone straight into the the fireplace, where it smashes and falls with an unsatisfying crack.

The demon inside of me emerges, and this time, I don't think there's will be any holding him back.

Fuck this little boy.

Daisy is mine.

GUNNAR

*W*ith a growl that makes my little Daisy gasp, I reach down and grab her forearm, tugging her up from the rug until she's standing.

I end up standing too, staring down at her, breathing hard and ragged as jealousy heats my veins. I struggle to get a hold of myself because the beast inside me wants to yell. To throw other things. But that would mean losing control ... and control is like my religion. To be in control, to master something ... there's a sense of satisfaction and pleasure that comes with it that's unlike anything else. I won't let that go. I wrangle the beast inside me back into his cage, promising him I'll deal with this. But not his way.

"Gunnar! What the hell is going on?" Daisy's shocked, staring at her phone, her free hand coming to her cheek in shock.

Her use of my real name only stirs me up more. *Gunnar? What happened to Daddy? Where the fuck did all our progress this morning go?*

"A date!" I growl in a low, controlled tone that belies the possessiveness burning through my system right now. "You have a fucking *date!*"

Her eyes widen, and her cheeks go pale, so I soften my hold on her arm because as angry as I am, I don't want her scared.

"Daddy is very upset right now, Daisy." My nostrils flare but I keep my breathing tight and controlled. "I thought you were my good girl."

"Daddy …." Her eyes are luminous as she stares up at me, breathing shallowly, unsure what to do—but I think—turned on. That same connection we had earlier clicks into place, like a key in a lock—the perfect fit.

Why would she ruin this perfect thing we've been building? The connection that's been budding between us, just about to bloom?

I refuse to let her ruin it.

I'm going to show her that she belongs to me. Always has, always will.

I drop my hold on her arm and sit down on the couch. With an icy tone that showcases my displeasure, I command, "Come here."

Her eyes study mine for a second, bouncing back and forth, trying to read my mood. "Now is not the time to be a brat. You've been bad. Bad girls get spanked."

I watch her intake of breath. The way her tight fists immediately loosen and how her tongue darts out to swipe across her lower lip.

Yes, you want this, Daisy. You know you do. Come here. You know you deserve to be punished.

She takes a hesitant step forward. Then another. When she's right in front of me, I grab her forearm and pull her down. She immediately settles across my lap, facedown on the couch, back arched, that luscious ass teasing me.

An ass she considered giving to someone else.

Oh, that makes my blood boil.

Yanking down her shorts and the flower-print panties beneath them, I'm still struck by how perfectly round her behind is when it's finally fully exposed to me. Soft and round, she has this perfect bubble butt. And she just walked over and surrendered to me.

A high even better than control starts to tangle with my anger. I fight to keep down both emotions because they aren't going to rule me right now. Not when I have to keep my focus and ride that line between dominance and going too far. I can't push too far.

"Do you deserve this spanking, Daisy? Tell me."

"Yes, sir." Her face is hidden in the couch cushions, but I know her. I've lived with her for over a year and watched her like a hawk that entire time, studying her, learning her. I know she's blushing like mad right now. But I can also see a little gap between her thighs, and the hint of her pussy lips. And the way the overhead lights are glinting off her cunt … she's *wet*.

I let my palm glide over her ass. God, it feels good in my hand. The skin is so pale and soft. I can't resist a single squeeze.

I shove my right arm across her back to hold her in place as I raise my left and bring it down. Hard.

She screeches and squirms, trying to use her arms to push up off the couch so she can get away from me. But I curl my fingers around her shoulder and dig in, spanking her three more times in rapid succession.

"I thought you were a good girl. You were supposed to be my good girl."

After another smack, I realize how pink her ass is getting. I can see my fingerprints. My mark on her. I like it. Heat travels down my spine at the sight and stirs in my dick.

Daisy tries pleading. "Stop. Daddy! I'm sorry. I didn't mean to say yes!"

"Are you lying, little flower?" I purr, making my tone soft to contrast the hard smacks I just gave her. "Did you want to go on a date with this boy? Let him kiss you? Let him see you in that outfit you tried to wear this morning?" I rub her ass cheek, palming it a little as I question her. She lets out a groan of pleasure and I immediately stop, because this spanking is about punishment, not pleasure.

"No. He asked … and I just froze up. I didn't mean to say yes. It popped out. I'm sorry." She groans, and her thighs shift, opening, inviting me in.

But instead of reaching between her thighs and giving her what she wants, I trail my hand softly up and down her ass, across her globes, near her crease … teasing her until she's gasping.

"You want attention, baby? Daddy will give you attention. All the attention you need." My tone is sensual but still dark. I'm angry at her for betraying this perfect thing between us, for being scared of it or questioning it or whatever made the word 'yes' tumble from her lips. But I'm even angrier at myself. Because after this morning, I'd thought things were clear. I thought we both knew we were headed in the same direction. I obviously didn't spell things out enough.

God, I can't believe she said yes to someone else. I want to wring this fucker's throat.

Who the hell dared to ask my girl out?

Molten rage courses through me and my heart is beating so fast it feels like I might have a heart attack. I can't be around her any longer. Not without doing something I'll regret. I release my arm from her back. When she doesn't climb off me, I gently slide over sideways, out from underneath her body. Daisy simply collapses, limp, on the couch as I stand up.

I charge from the room, the drive to expel this fury overwhelming me. I don't see where I'm going, not really. My feet move on autopilot until I find myself in the basement, staring at my gym equipment. I have to purge this demon. I have to get rid of this pulsing anger somehow and I can't keep taking it out on her.

I expected too much from her. We'd established too little. And that little fucker … God, he had the worst timing.

I don't bother strapping on safety gear. I just drop my suit pants so that I'm in boxers and rip off my collared shirt so that all that's left is the white tee underneath. Then I move to the punching bag. If I fuck up and break my own wrist—well, then, I deserve it.

Stupid fucking fool.

We should have had a talk this morning.

I shouldn't have left things simmering. I should have brought them to a boil and made things crystal clear. I should have eaten my girl out until she screamed. Just lifted her up on that kitchen counter and yanked down her jeans and panties … sent her to school soaked, thighs still trembling from an orgasm.

Then the word yes never would have spilled from her gorgeous lips.

I start with some simple jab-cross combos, gradually speeding up until I have a rhythm that matches my furiously pounding heart.

Words my mother said to me decades ago float up to haunt me.

I'd been eight or something when my little brother had screwed up a make-believe battle we were staging in the backyard. I'd freaked out and punched him—gave him a black eye. Mom had pulled me into the dining room, her brown eyes serious and scolding as she'd said, "Gunnar, you have these expectations for people. And sometimes, they're not realistic. Sometimes people don't understand what you want. Sometimes, they can't give you exactly what you want. Your brother isn't a little robot you can control. He's his own person."

I'd thought my mother was an idiot.

But here I am, forty-fucking-two, expecting Daisy to be every fucking thing I want and freaking out because I misread a few happy glances and thought we were on the same page without sitting down and having a conversation … like a goddamned fool.

I've been building this up too much. It's my fault. My fault. Sneaking into her bedroom all those nights only built up all my lust, made me fail to think clearly. I've been fantasizing about her so long that when the time came to change fantasy to reality, I choked. I didn't take that step. I'm too used to sneaking. Subtlety. I've come to love that too much over the time I've known her because for so long, it's all I've had.

The night is silent, except for the whirr of Darla's oxygen machine. I stride down the hall in bare feet, thankful for the way the thick carpeting muffles my steps as I go check on her. I push open the very first door at the top of the stairs. She's asleep in her bedroom, her eyes closed, the moonlight painting her dark hair silver, wan and sunken cheeks made even sharper by the shadows. During the day, Darla plays at being calm and peaceful, though she knows that the clock is her enemy. But at night, her hands cross peacefully over her chest and the lines around her mouth relax. She almost looks like she's smiling.

Guilt nudges me at the sight of her, tells me that Darla trusts me and I should go to sleep in the master suite down the hall. But I've become adept at side-stepping that pesky emotion. It's minuscule in comparison to the lust that's racing through my system right now.

I've had three surgeries and dozens of consults holding me back. I haven't been able to have special time with my Daisy all week.

But I will tonight. She won't know it, but we're going to have some very special time together.

Already half-stiff at the thought, I carefully pull the door to Darla's bedroom shut, slowly releasing the knob so that even the click of the latch is nearly silent.

Then I walk to the next room. Daisy's door is shut but never locked and I sneak in without bothering to close it behind me—in case I need to make a quick escape. My sweet girl isn't the heaviest sleeper. But that only adds to the thrill for me, to see what I can do without getting caught.

Tonight is a very lucky night—it's warm and she's kicked the covers into a little tangle around her creamy legs. Curled on her side, she's wearing a pink tank top and that ass of hers is clad in a lace-lined pair of silky white panties. Her night-light ensures that I can clearly see the crease between those creamy cheeks.

One day, I'm going to plug you there, little flower, *I think as I reach into my sweatpants and pull out my cock. It's already at half-mast, and when the cool air from her ceiling fan hits it, it just becomes more sensitive.* Daddy's going to buy you a cute little plug and prep your ass. And then he's going to fuck it.

It doesn't take much to stroke myself to hardness, not when I haven't visited Daisy in awhile. The soft skin of her thighs holds my attention and I wonder when the last time she masturbated was.

I stop jerking myself for a minute and walk over to her hamper in the corner, next to the door that leads to her bathroom. Sometimes, I can find drenched panties inside her collection of dirty clothes, and that's when I know she's been naughty.

Shuffling through the tank tops and shorts, I find two pairs of panties. One is a disappointing blue pair without any stain on the crotch, but the other is a gold mine. A silky purple thong with a gusset that's still slightly damp.

I bring it up to my nose and inhale. Fuck. Yes. I love the tangy, forbidden scent of her.

I bring the silk down and use it to rub my cock, imagining that she's still wearing these panties, that I'm in bed behind her, my dick between her lush thighs, sliding up and down against this purple silk as I try to convince her to let me fuck her.

"Please, let Daddy in. Just for a second, baby."

"It's wrong. People will say things. Hate us!" Her voice comes out breathy inside my imagination, just like it did the first time we met.

"It's not wrong. We need each other. We make each other feel good. Let me make you feel good." Fuck. God. The depravity of that role-play heats my blood and makes it course like a river, straight to my fucking dick, which swells against my hand. "Don't you love me, baby?"

"Yes." Her voice is soft.

"Then let me in."

I reach up with my left hand and lick a stripe up my palm as I drop the panties from my right, imagining I just shoved them aside. Then I fuck my wet left hand, squeezing tight, pretending it's her pussy.

I stare at her figure as I do it, watching as she turns in her sleep, her tank top pulling tight so that the top of her left areola is exposed—so soft and rosy. Perfect for me to suck.

It doesn't take me long to come—spurting all over my hand.

Then I tuck myself back into my pants and steal away, knowing I'll be back another night … until one day fantasy can become reality.

"You stupid fuck," I curse myself, breathing hard as I move from punching to kicking. I smash the side of my foot into the bag, watching it sway. "You should have just asked her out the day you met—"

She would have said no. She wasn't in any mental space to date. Or she would have said yes and then pulled away when her mother took a turn for the worse. But also … the dark and depraved part of me wouldn't have liked simple dating as much. The sicko inside of me wanted to be her daddy …

actually live out that filthy scenario that started unfurling inside my head the moment I met her.

I couldn't bring myself to do it while Darla was around. Not outright anyway.

But now, she's saying yes to dates with other guys ... and I wonder if, underneath it all, I've fucked things up.

I smash the bag until it feels like my limbs are on fire. I smash until my legs are quaking underneath me. Until my throat is parched and screaming for water. Until my rage has gone limp, and I'm less likely to commit a felony if I learn this Justin-fucker's last name.

I drag my ass up to the kitchen. I fill a cup with water and drain it before moving to the front hall, wanting to glance at the key hooks on the wall by the front door. Did Daisy leave? Did she run?

Goddammit, maybe she did. Maybe I pushed too fast with the spanking? I should have stayed there and talked to her afterward. What the fuck kind of Dom am I? Apparently reading eighty fucking articles and watching endless porn on the subject does not translate into skills. I'm pissed at myself. I hate fucking mistakes and I think I made one just now by leaving to go expel all my anger without talking to her first.

But her Mustang keys are still on the hook. Her red leather purse is still sitting on the hall table.

I blink at the sight, trying to process what I'm seeing.

She must have locked herself in her room then.

I sigh. I need to apologize for leaving her, for not doing after care, for neglecting her, and not verifying she felt safe even during punishment.

I refill my water glass and trudge toward the stairs. But as I walk by the living room, I stop short. And it's not at the sight of the scene of my crime, the couch cushions that are still indented from our combined weight. No. I'm shocked into stillness by the vision of Daisy, standing at the opposite end of the room by the bookshelf, her shorts still pulled down around her thighs, her ass exposed the way I left it, her face pressed against the corner.

Did I traumatize her that much when I left? Is she in shock?

Those thoughts drop onto me like an anvil, crushing me with the knowledge that I might have broken her. My sweet, lovely Daisy. The person I adore most in the world. I'm a fucking monster.

How can I fix this? What can I do? She looks fucking comatose right now, unmoving. Shit.

I take a cautious step into the room, not wanting her to think I'm threatening her in any way. I keep my distance, and also leave a path to the doorway clear in case she feels like she needs to run. Leaning sideways so that she can see my face if she turns hers, I call out, "Daisy?"

Her face turns slowly in my direction and that's when I see the tear tracks that stain her cheeks. I did that. I made her cry. I watch as she blinks, and slowly opens her mouth.

I expect her to scream or cry or call me a bastard. I don't expect what she actually says.

"Daddy, I'm sorry I made you mad. I put myself in timeout."

DAISY

*M*y hands are planted against the walls, nose inches from the corner, my body is quivering with excitement and trepidation. I don't think I've ever done anything this forward in my life.

There's a long moment where Gunnar just stares at me and I think during that short expanse of time that he feels about eighty thousand different things. I can't identify all of the micro emotions but I'm certain I see shock and skepticism in there before he lands on pure unadulterated lust.

Nerves spiral inside my belly as he strides over to me and I feel my neck heat up.

Is this actually happening? Oh my God, I think it might be. Based on the spanking thing, I'd leaned into playing up the daddy kink we've been toying with—taking a calculated risk by putting my nose in the corner.

Waiting for him to come back up was one of the most agonizing things I've ever done in my life. I second-guessed myself dozens of times. I cried. I felt guilty. I nearly grabbed my keys and drove off to avoid facing him and this entire scenario.

But I kept dragging my ass back to the corner because I want Gunnar more than I've ever wanted anyone. Because I regret blurting out yes to that random guy. Because I clearly hurt Gunnar and I need to atone. This is the only way I can think of that might get through to him.

I was shocked by the spanking thing ... and even more surprised to realize how much I liked it.

I need him to know that I want this dynamic and *him*. I've wanted him for so long, though I've tried to tell myself time after time that it's wrong, but now the need to explore the chemistry between us is like electricity flowing just beneath my skin. I have to know what it can be like between us. I can't go on wondering.

Even the fact that it's forbidden turns me on.

The idea of others knowing about us—what they'll say, how they'll judge, the disgusted looks we'll get—that certainly still freaks me out and sets my teeth on edge. But not more than the utter heartbreak I saw in his eyes the moment he read that text.

As Gunnar walks toward me, I feel the air change, the room heat up, and anticipation makes my thighs clench.

Fuck, I'm so glad I stayed here and chose this. It looks like it's paying off. I think it's paying off. I hope so. Feathers tickle the insides of my throat and I kind of want to giggle in relief at the break in this tension between us.

When he gets close his presence washes over me before I can even hear his breathing. He's just so dominant that whenever I'm in his sphere ... it's like entering nuclear territory; it infects my very cells, transforming them. And the sight of Gunnar so sweaty and unkempt, his shirt plastered to his chest, does things to me.

He's already half undressed, wearing only boxers and a t-shirt, and I'm … nearly there. He can have me naked in seconds. The idea of Gunnar taking me is so much more satisfying than the discussion at lunch earlier today, when the girls had suggested I give it up just to get it over with.

No. This will be so much better.

Gunnar's hand comes to rest on my lower back, sending a flush immediately up my system and making my spine stiffen in awareness. I forget to breathe as his voice curls around my ear, low and sultry. "First of all, Daddy needs to say he's sorry for losing his temper. You made him jealous."

That admission of jealousy does far more for me than the apology. Yes, those spankings *hurt,* but the idea that Gunnar Strong flew into a rage because he was fucking jealous—over me—an incandescent glow flares inside my lower belly and all the butterflies in my stomach are drawn toward that light, fluttering down, down, down. I clench my thighs.

"I'm sorry. It was a mistake. I won't do it again," I promise breathily.

"Mmmm," he murmurs, as his palm skates down over my still-bared ass, rubbing lightly over the marks he made. My skin tingles in awareness, slightly sore still but that's nothing compared to the fact that he's touching me there. "You'd better not."

"I won't. I'm yours."

"Say that again," he whispers.

"I'm yours."

His sharp inhale makes me so euphoric that tears come to my eyes.

My hands come up to clutch futilely at the wall as Gunnar gently strokes a fingertip down the crease of my ass. God, how many times have I guiltily dreamed of him touching me like this? I resist the urge to lift up onto my tiptoes and arch my back so that he can see how wet a few words and a simple touch have gotten me. He nearly drove me insane earlier on the couch.

I bite my lower lip hard, teeth digging in. *Patience,* I tell myself. *He's almost there.*

His finger dips to the underside of the curve of my ass and I automatically tense in anticipation. But he doesn't touch me *there*. His fingertip never reaches my throbbing sex. It disappears.

I give the tiniest whimper.

He shushes me, breath blowing against the shell of my ear as he slides my panties and then my sleep shorts back up, covering me. A little knot of disappointment tightens in my belly because I'd kind of hoped that he'd throw me down and claim me. But instead, he's gently turning me, pulling my hands down from the wall and interlocking our fingers.

I stare up at him, panting and dazed, not understanding what he's doing—if this is rejection or something else.

He raises our linked hands and plants a kiss on each one of my knuckles. Each brush of his lips makes the tension between us build up, crackling like static electricity inside a cloud—the precursor to a lightning bolt.

But the lightning doesn't come. Gunnar doesn't step forward and seal our lips together or grab me roughly and pin me to the wall.

He turns, leading me back to the couch. I try not to trip over my own feet as I follow, bewildered.

He doesn't sit back in *the* spot, but at the other end, near the arm. I'm surprised when he pulls me down onto his lap sideways, however. My ass aches a little bit at the contact. But the fact that he's quickly wrapping those huge arms around me, pulling me in so that my head settles into the crook of his neck, sends such a warm ray of sunshine through me that I hardly notice the pain.

"We need to talk," he utters the classic bad news phrase and my throat dries out. "God, Daisy," his fingers flex and dig into my skin for a moment before he releases. "I'm fucking obsessed with you."

Smug delight curls up the corners of my lips and I place a hand over his racing heart. I can feel the sturdy thudding through his white t-shirt. "Same," I whisper. "It makes me feel guilty—"

"Don't. Don't ever feel guilty. Feelings just are. They just happen."

I nod, not meeting his eyes.

"I've thought about nothing but you for almost two years, Daisy." He turns my head and pushes his lips against mine, that five o'clock shadow of his scratching deliciously against my face as he nips at my lower lip. My worries dissolve when his teeth drop that lip and then own my mouth with a dominating kiss.

Our first kiss.

And oh God, it's perfect.

Our tongues tangle and tease, mine tentative and exploring, before his starts roughly fucking my mouth—showing me exactly what he's going to do next.

I melt into him, and as his hands dig into my hips, I twine my hands through his salt-sprinkled chestnut hair. It's just as soft as I always imagined it would be. I run my fingers gently through it at first, but as the kiss climbs in intensity, I end up yanking on the top where it's longer.

I might be a little too rough, because Gunnar pulls back with a chuckle, out of breath but smiling down at me in a way that makes my heart skip like a stone across a pond, defying gravity.

"Daisy. I want you so much. But sweetheart, I need to tell you that I … like certain things. Things you may not be able to give me. Or find too twisted."

"I won't!" I rush to answer him. "I want to give you whatever you want."

He groans and then laughs. "God, to hear you say that. But first, I need to spell it out."

"How about you spell it out with your tongue on my tongue while I try to figure it out? It'll be like a game." I propose with a saucy wink.

His hand leaves my breast, falling back down to my waist to encircle me. I'm left panting, wanting, my sensitive breast aching for more of his touch as his arms tighten around me in a hug. I jut out my lower lip and pout.

"Let me finish, baby girl, or you'll end up back in timeout."

I press my lips together. Considering how disappointing it was to be taken out of timeout just now when I thought I'd get pinned against the wall, I don't want to repeat that experience. I want whatever other dirty things Gunnar's thinking of instead.

He speaks slowly, and part of me wants to shake him until he just spits out the words. But this is clearly hard for him.

"Since the first day I saw you … I've wanted … I want a different kind of relationship with you. And it's not because I don't love you. I just … I crave things that aren't normal. From you."

I lick my lips in anticipation, though I feel like I already have an inkling about what he's going to say. "Like what?"

"First of all, submission."

I burst into giggles that rattle my entire ribcage, mirth overtaking me. Oh my God. He's ridiculous. Gunnar has to wait until I catch a gasping breath before I can explain. "You think that's a revelation? That's not just from me. You want everyone to do what you say. You're a total control freak."

He grins and traces his index finger up the inside of my arm. "True. That's true. But I want sexy submission from you. And more control over you than I want over anyone else."

"Okay," I breathe, loving his use of the word sexy submission. Immediately I picture myself kneeling for him. I like that idea—like it a lot. "I'll do what you say."

"You'll have a safe word, of course—"

"Pineapple. Has to be pineapple."

He shakes his head and then reaches up to cup my cheek. "It can be whatever you want."

I lean into his palm, staring at his eyes, still slightly shocked that we're actually having this conversation. "So … do you want me to kneel for you?"

"We're not done talking." His tone is calm, but beneath my ass, his dick twitches inside his boxers and I know he likes my offer. "I have more kinks."

"More?" *Oh, do tell.* I rub my thighs together, enjoying the way it sends a tingle up my spine that matches the delightful anticipation coursing through my veins right now.

He takes a deep breath, as if this next part is hard for him to admit. But his eyes are steady on mine as he admits, "Secrecy. Part of my kink is the idea of sneaking around. Both of us role-playing like we're sneaking around … and also me … following you. Watching you."

A little bit of shock rolls through me. That's a lot to take in. But as I absorb it, the secrecy part feels a lot like what we're already doing. And the idea of Gunnar's eyes devouring me— well that, I just straight up love.

"So, don't tell anyone what we're doing?" I give a shaky laugh. "I don't really know how I'd explain it anyway." I can only imagine the shocked look on Rose's face. Lily might get it. Violet … I'm not sure if she would. She's been promised by her family to some old guy she's never even met. She'd probably think I'm crazy.

Realistically, we won't be able to keep this thing a secret forever, but for now … sure.

"You're okay with me following you?" His tone is tight. "Think it through."

"Um … in case you haven't noticed, my life consists of home and the animal shelter. Now school. I'm not that thrilling. So, yeah, if you want to hide behind the animal cages and smell dog shit …"

"Let me be more specific. I want to record you on video. I want to watch you. I want to jerk off in your room at night standing over you. Newsflash, I've done that one. But I also want to follow you and tell you all sorts of naughty things to do in public while I watch."

Oh. Oh. Damn. I stare at Gunnar, reeling a little. Trying to process this. It's a bit of an overload. "You've jerked off in my room?"

"With your panties."

I fight a blush as I confess, "I've done it on your bed before while you were at work." Instinctively, I want to hide my face, because that's a secret I thought I'd take to the grave.

"Ugh. God. Daisy." He squeezes my thigh. "You're so fucking perfect, baby."

His praise makes me giddy.

"So … um … anything else? Blood play or animal sacrifices?" I tease.

He gives me a stern look. "Are you making fun of me?"

"If I am, will you spank me again?"

"Did you like it?" He looks genuinely curious.

I give a little thought to the answer before I respond. "I deserved it. But, yeah, I also kinda liked it." With anyone else, I'd be embarrassed to admit that, but after he's just disclosed all of these things, I find myself feeling brave enough to be vulnerable too and tell him what I want. "I kind of want you to spank me and then slide that hand down and finger me until I scream."

"Mmmm … Daisy. You are the most perfect woman ever invented."

My heart skips and I bring my hand to his chest, happy to feel that his is beating just as quickly as mine. "Does that mean yes?"

"Oh, no." He shakes his head steadily, though his eyes dance with banked heat. His five-o'clock shadow makes him look twice as intimidating and severe as normal. "I think you're forgetting my first kink, princess. I'm the boss."

I cross my arms as best I can while on his lap and stick my tongue out.

He just grins. "You want to play? We can play. But we're going to do it my way."

His thumbs edge up my inner thighs, brushing against the hem of my sleep shorts and I'm desperate for him to keep going. There's a low, aching pulse in my pussy. And finally, it's going to be satisfied.

"Yes. Please." I have no idea what to expect even though he spelled out all his rules. Does he want to watch me right now? Because I could make myself come in about two seconds flat. I've never been this turned on before in my life. Or does he want to try out some role-play? Some kind of exhibition? I'm dying to know. And I'm all on board for Gunnar's kinks—whatever it takes. As long as I get to keep calling him Daddy, which he seems to like, I'm good.

"Then stand up, pretty girl." His hands release me and I pop right up, standing, ready for anything. Does he want to go to the bedroom? Will he be into handcuffs and all that Fifty

Shades shit? Possibilities flicker through my head as he stands behind me and towers over me.

I look up at him, for the millionth time admiring his size. Those broad shoulders I want to bite and mark, the dark hair speckled with gray—currently looking windswept because he was downstairs. I even like the little patch of sweat on his white tee that clings to his happy trail. For the first time ever, I let my eyes drift down to the very obvious tent in his black boxers. It looks big. God.

"Gunnar," I whisper, "You know I'm a virgin, right?" I'm not just playing into his fantasy right now … I really, really need him to know that he can't just plow right into me. My eyes travel up to his deep brown gaze, and he must realize I'm serious. I quickly explain, "I mean … I've got a dildo and stuff. I'm not, like, totally, um … you know what, I'm going to stop talking." I blush, all my earlier confidence asking for a spanking fading, though I have no idea why.

"Fuck." Gunnar reaches out and grabs my jaw roughly. And then his lips are on mine, claiming me again—roughly. This isn't a sweet kiss; it's a kiss of raw possession as his lips close over mine and his tongue darts out, pushing past my lips and savagely plundering my mouth.

It's so fucking good that my mind floats away, and my knees threaten to collapse.

But, just as quickly as he started, he pulls away, dropping my chin and stepping back.

After a moment spent collecting my wits, I blink up at him, worried I did something wrong.

"I'm going to shower. You make popcorn and pick a movie for us to watch."

Wait. What? What is happening? My eyes trail after him as he strides toward the front hall. I'm literally a panting, soaking wet mess right now.

He turns in the archway and glances back at me, a cold smile crossing his face. "Rule number one: don't touch yourself. Daddy will know."

As he disappears, I press my thighs together. Fuck. As if him saying that didn't just make me goddamned hotter. *What did I just agree to?* I squeeze my thighs together where I stand. It's torture. *But delicious torture,* I remind myself, *and so much better than what you've been doing to yourself for the last year.*

I drift into the kitchen, still wading through this new reality that I can't quite believe as I grab a bag of popcorn and stuff it into the microwave.

I start to anticipate the way Gunnar will look when he comes back down. Will he bother tossing new boxers on? Or will he just yell down the stairs for me to come up? Will I get to see him with water droplets sticking to his chest, dripping from the tips of his dark hair? Or will he dry off and stroke himself, staring in the mirror, before he comes back down to me?

Bed? Or couch? He did say movie night, but I don't really believe him. Movies mean dark rooms and wandering hands, which will definitely turn into more. The question is whether he can make it all the way downstairs first and wait for me to press play. I fucking hope not.

The scent of buttered popcorn fills the kitchen as the microwave finishes up, dinging. I cut some strawberries at the island butcher block table to go with the popcorn because Gunnar always likes some sweet with his salty, but he won't do processed sugar. I also pour us each a glass of water.

I bring everything to the coffee table and set it out before flipping on the TV to settle on a show. I pick an action flick that I have zero interest in because I won't mind missing it. I get it all set up to play, and when I glance over toward the open archway to check for Gunnar, I see my broken phone on the ground. I walk over and pick it up. The screen is cracked and not just a little. There's a whole lot of nothing on the screen. It's a goner.

"I'm sorry about that. I ordered you a new one. Should get delivered tomorrow." Gunnar's voice makes me spin around.

He doesn't look like any of my naughty fantasy predictions. He's not naked, his massive biceps and chest on display for me. He's not in just a towel so I can peek at his happy trail. He's dressed in a loose t-shirt and pajama pants, just like he wears to bed every winter night.

He didn't shave, so his chiseled, dimpled chin is lined with the dark, delicious scruff I've come to love seeing every night. But his hair is slicked back, and everything about him looks so disappointingly … normal.

"Thanks," I mumble around the disappointment sitting like a marble inside my mouth. It's hard to care about a phone when all you want is to be thrown down and deflowered. Why is he dressed?

"What'd you pick? Oh, nice choice. Come on, sweetie. Sit next to me." He casually plops down on the couch and reaches for a slice of strawberry, popping it into his mouth.

I swear I could knit a sweater out of the nerves unraveling inside me right now. I debate whether I should be acting innocent or sultry to put him in the mood and I swear I just glitch out and end up awkward. "Okay!" I bound over far too enthusiastically.

I see him suppress a smile, trying not to laugh at me. He knows I have no clue what I'm doing though, what does he expect?

Embarrassed, I end up sitting too far away.

"I don't bite," he jokes, and I scoot over until he wraps his arm around my shoulder.

I can't even begin to describe how that feels. That classic moment from every romance movie ever, where the guy stretches his arm around the girl, casually claiming her. It helps the fretful embarrassment ease, and I snuggle next to him as he presses play.

I pay absolutely no mind to the movie. All of my attention is on Gunnar's left hand, which strokes my shoulder, then plays with my hair, then slowly skates up and down my arm.

What is he doing? Is he making this like a movie date? Where are all the ravaging kisses from before?

Part of me wants to make a move, but after the practically-skipping-to-the-couch debacle, I don't want to fuck up the mood further. So I bite my lip and sit patiently, attempting to enjoy each little touch.

Slowly, I realize what I think he's doing. He's playing sneaky. Fuck. God. Why is that hot? Playing forbidden? I mean, we're already about as forbidden as it gets in society's eyes, but the fact that he's trying to be so subtle, to build this sensual suspense ... I might burst into flame.

It feels like it takes an eternity before he finally caresses the side of my breast. At first, it's so slight that it seems accidental, but over time, his fingertips drag up and down over my shirt more deliberately. They get closer and closer to my nipple, but don't quite touch it.

Fuck. It must be forty-five minutes into the movie and he's still barely playing. I think he's trying to kill me.

Anticipation coils inside of me and I dig my fingers into the couch cushion as his forefinger and thumb finally move to pinch my stiff nipple through my sleep shirt. The effect is immediate. Like a final railroad spike that finishes off the tracks that have already been laid, the simple tug he gives makes me pant and arch. More, I need more.

I turn toward him and bring my lips to his neck, but he pulls back, his face turning away from the movie he's been pretending to watch in order to glare down at me. "Rule two: Daddy initiates play time."

Fuck. Was this not initiated? What counts as initiated? But he's already turned back to the movie, his fingers still pinching my nipple through my shirt and tugging rhythmically. It feels so good but … it's not enough. It's a lit match when I want a fucking campfire.

I stare at the screen, where blurry figures move around—shouting and chasing each other in flashy cars no real person would ever own. Is this what being a submissive means? It's more intense than I expected. In both good and bad ways. I want to yell at him. But I also am nearly delirious with desire right now. I swear the couch beneath me is going to be a ruined soggy mess.

I try to breathe evenly and keep calm, letting Gunnar take the lead. It's hard though. Even though my eyes are locked on the TV, all of my awareness is focused on Gunnar's right hand.

In my peripheral vision, I can see him reaching for something.

A throw blanket is tossed across our laps and he whispers, "Thought you might be cold."

Cold? Are you kidding? I want to laugh at how ridiculous that statement is as he pinches hard and another trail of heat slides down my spine to pulse futilely in my core. But, with the throw blanket covering me, I can at least squeeze my thighs, try to subtly rub my legs together.

"Nuh-uh. Spread those legs, baby," he whispers.

Dammit.

I open slightly, pouting, hoping his other hand will slide underneath the blanket and search out my clit, through my shorts, under my shorts—I don't fucking care. I'm just desperate to be touched.

"Please," I beg quietly.

"Please, what? Use your words."

"Please touch me. I need your fingers."

The fingers from his free hand come to my knee, circling there. "Better?" he asks in a low murmur.

That fucking smartass. Oh, I want to smack him. But then I won't get what I want. I lick my lips and pant as he tugs a little quicker at my nipple, pulling my breast up and letting it fall with each tiny tug—more intense than before. More evil.

"God, please touch my pussy." I can't help how my voice gets a little shrill. I'm desperate.

"Shhh." He shushes me and glances toward the door.

I knew we were sneaking. Fuck. Fuck. How am I supposed to keep quiet?

After a minute, he turns from the movie and stares down at me. "Who do you want to touch your pussy?" he coaches. His brown eyes are a deep melted chocolate that ensnares me.

"Daddy, will you please touch my pussy?"

He gives a soft hum of approval, and his hand slides up from my knee dragging over the skin of my inner thigh. I suck in a breath when his fingers dive beneath the opening in the leg of my shorts. I whimper when he pulls aside the soaked panties that are clinging to me.

"So wet." He whispers as his finger glides over my folds.

My back arches a tiny bit at his touch—I've been waiting so damn long for it that it nearly undoes me. He slides up and down, up and down, mapping the curves, spreading my lips, tracing the soft insides before moving his slickened fingers up to gently circle my clit.

I'm going to explode. My thoughts are tumbling like rocks down a mountain cliff and shattering into little pebbles. Nothing exists but this feeling of falling—my hips start to buck.

"No, princess. Someone might see. Stay still, or I won't get to finish."

Goddamn it ... I think this might be harder than submission. Shit.

I pant, stilling my hips, fingers digging into the cushion to the point of pain. Oh, I might fucking smack him if he makes me wait much—

He pinches my clit, tugging.

I combust. I explode into a million tiny little pieces. Oh. My. God. I fight not to move my hips but my feet end up kicking at the couch—I can't control my bucking, though I do bite on my lip to stop the sounds that want to erupt. I become a silent, writhing mess. Gunnar doesn't let go like he threatened; he keeps tugging, pinching my nipple harder, drawing out the pleasure that has my head turning side to side.

Oh, God.

Oh my God.

I flop backward, boneless, when the quivers stop crackling through my nerve-endings. I'm panting. I'm glowing. A gentle smile graces my face.

He leans down and murmurs in my ear. "Did Daddy make you feel good, baby?"

I nod limply. "So good."

His hands retreat from my body then, carefully replacing my panties. The hand that just stroked me to orgasm comes up to his lips and I watch as he tastes me. "Mmm. The perfect bedtime snack."

He's so filthy. I fucking love it. Even this kink—which I wasn't sure about while we tried it. I don't think I would have come so hard if he hadn't riled me to the point of fury.

"Speaking of bedtime, you have class tomorrow. Get upstairs."

Wait. What?

My afterglow vanishes as he removes his arm from around my shoulders. He pushes the blanket off his lap onto mine and stands to clean up the snacks that only he ate.

"But … but … sex?" I ask weakly. Why are there bowls in his hands right now when he should be grabbing onto me? Throwing me down on the couch?

He turns, giving me a sharp look. "Daisy. What did I tell you about secrets?" His voice is a harsh whisper, and he lets his gaze wander deliberately to the door then back.

Oh, we're still playing. Sneaking. Secrecy. Okay, good. Relief floods me at the realization that we aren't done.

My lips snap together and I lower my gaze repentantly for a second before batting my eyelashes as I look back up at him. "Sorry. Sorry. Do you need help cleaning up?" I'm so giddy right now that I struggle to stop myself from bouncing on my toes because Gunnar Strong is going to fuck me.

"Just fold your blanket and head upstairs. I'll get the rest."

I'm dazed as I follow his instructions, wondering what's going to happen next. What's Daddy going to do?

DAISY

*H*e put me to bed. In my own fucking room. He tucked me in, kissed me goodnight, and then left—that bastard!

I lay in the dark on my side, facing my window and fuming. The light pollution from the city spoils any view of the stars but I can see the Sandia mountains looming over us, deep blue and solid in the distance. Normally, I love the sight of them. Not tonight. Tonight, I'm nothing short of pissed. Way to rile a girl up and leave her hanging.

Okay, I technically got an orgasm—but just *one*? I was not ready to be done. I didn't even get to touch his dick! Gunnar wasn't lying when he said he was sick and twisted, or that he wanted control.

He reminded me about rule number one again before he shut my door.

He doesn't want me touching myself—as if it's possible to resist after what just happened. Fucking hell, just the memory of the way his profile looked, his face lit up blue by the light of the TV, all serious and intent on the movie while his hands slid over my body and did naughty things, makes me ache with need all over ….

This must be what he meant about saying I might not be into his kinks. Ugh. Self denial? Really? This rule … I don't know if I like this part of submission.

My hand starts to slide down my belly. I can't help it. What he wants is impossible. There's no way I can follow the no touching myself rule. I could probably have ten orgasms thinking about what we did tonight and it still wouldn't be enough. I cup my panties, which are soaked. I'm dragging the heel of my hand down the front when I hear my door knob turn.

Immediately, my hand flies back up to clutch at my pillow. *Dammit! Is he fucking psychic? Does he have a hidden camera—oh shit, why does that make me even wetter? Do I like the idea of him spying on me?*

I feel a dull throb down below. Apparently, yes I do.

Is he here to punish me then? Does he know?

My stomach tightens, and I stop breathing, anticipation turning me into a statue as he steps inside.

"Daisy. Are you asleep? Daddy needs to talk to you." He used that word. Our playtime word.

As he shuts my door, my limbs unlock, and my stomach swoops in excitement as I realize the entire bedtime routine was a ploy. This is even better than getting caught touching myself and earning a spanking. Gunnar's sneaking into my room to toy with me.

Fuck his sneaking kink. But also ... damn. There's nobody even here to catch us but it doesn't matter. My body reacts like there is. Like there are other people in the house, guests in every bedroom. My fury melts, bubbles into excitement, boils into steam, and clouds the air with lust.

Each step he takes across the carpet makes my heart speed up until it's a quick trilling thump against my ribs.

I roll over to face him, putting on a sleepy voice. "Daddy?"

The bed dips as he sits down on the edge. His hand reaches up and he caresses my cheek. "I can't sleep, little flower. And you're in trouble because it's all your fault."

"My fault?" *Shit. He did see me!* I try to hide my guilt by contorting my face in mock confusion.

He nods solemnly, reaching for one of my arms and pulling my hand out from underneath the covers. Luckily, it's not the one I was using on myself, but as he drags it closer I wonder if he's going to check my hands. Fuck. I try to subtly wipe the other hand on the fitted sheet. I didn't go beneath my panties, but they were drenched, and I have no doubt there's evidence there.

But my frantic cover-up is all for nothing because he turns slightly to better face me and plants our joined hands over his erection. The stiff line tenting his pajama pants is thick and warm and wider than I expected. As Gunnar moves his hand to place it on top of mine and make me rub up and down his length, I realize he's wider than half my palm.

Gunnar's tone is pure sex as he groans at my touch. Then he says, "You made me hard, baby. I can't sleep like this. So you're going to have to take care of this problem." His eyes are shadowed and hard to make out, but I can see the creases at the end of them grow deeper when he smiles a dirty, vicious smile—the type I've never seen from him before. It steals my breath away because it's both intimate and intimidating.

I'm not even play-acting when I ask, "What do you want me to do?" Right now, with the way he's staring at me, I'd do anything. Anything.

"Get on your knees and face me," he orders as he pulls away from my hand and stands.

I quickly follow his instructions, tossing aside my quilt and kneeling sideways on the bed.

My eyes devour him as he whips off his shirt and then his sleep pants. He's so fucking fit, and the veins in his forearms seem to be even more defined in the harsh shadows of night. His nipples are dark and pebbled, peeking out from the patch of chest hair. He pulls off the brand-new boxers he put on less than an hour ago, and finally I get to see it.

His dick is darker than the rest of his skin, swollen, with a thick mushroom tip already leaking precum. It's already full mast, and knowing I made it that way makes me clench my thighs.

Gunnar walks forward with purpose, commanding, "Kiss it the way you kissed me earlier, baby."

He stops, standing right in front of me on the side of the bed, and I lean forward, putting my hands on the mattress, tilting my head down, and opening my lips to kiss the tip. I swirl my tongue experimentally, tasting him. His precum is salty and I lap at his slit to get all of it before sliding further down onto him, rewarded by his surprised grunt.

I've given blowjobs before—but those feel like a million years ago—and I can't really say I've got much technique. But Gunnar's full of whispered instructions and encouragement, which makes me feel like I'm doing a good job for him.

"God, that's it, baby girl. Use those sweet thick lips and seal them around me. Suck it hard. Oh, you're being soo good for Daddy. You're making me feel so good. Fuck." He reaches down over my back and his big fingers land on my ass—start to knead it roughly through my pajama shorts. His manhandling makes me desperate, and I long to touch myself. I try to slide up to ask him for permission, but he bucks further into my mouth, taking control of me. Using me. He doesn't push all the way into my throat, going easy on me, but he does test my limits until I have to yank my head back and gasp for air.

When I do, I meet his eyes. They're a chocolate inferno. I maintain eye contact as I slowly slide back onto the tip and suck lightly, tonguing the underside.

My nipples have never been this hard. My body's never been so tightly strung. But I've gotten an orgasm already. He hasn't. I should wait. It's only fair. Plus, if I want my next one to be half as good as the last one, I should definitely wait. That was mind-meltingly good.

I try to relax my throat so he can get farther in, which he does. He pulls my ass cheeks apart, digs his fingers into the crack, and holds me in place as he fucks my mouth.

"This ass. I've stared at this every day. Every fucking day, it's been so hard not to just take you. But now you're mine, baby. You hear me? Those lips belong to me. On my cock. I'm never going to let you go. Daisy. Baby, I'm going to come!" He warns me right before his cock jerks and spasms, shooting warm liquid onto my tongue. I do my best to swallow, but he comes a lot, twitching and pulsing as he pistons in and out, and some cum escapes the corners of my mouth, dripping down my chin.

Gunnar pulls out slowly with a sigh, gazing down at me with a sort of dazed tenderness I've never seen from anyone before. His hand reaches over to cup my cheek, and I half expect him to scold me for not swallowing it all, but he just stares at me glassy-eyed for a moment before whispering, "You're amazing."

Be still my heart. Most guys mutter a "thank you" or immediately worry about cleaning themselves up, at least in my limited experience. But he's praising me—with that look that makes me feel like I'm levitating. What is that look?

He does turn from me then. He bends and reaches for his t-shirt, scooping it up off the floor and wrapping it around his fingers before using a small corner of the hem to carefully dab at my chin, wiping me up with a gentleness that contrasts the bruises that are likely forming on my ass right now. He grabs the cup of water I always keep on my nightstand overnight and offers it to me.

As I drink, I watch him silently, wondering what he'll do next. We're well past the point where I'm going to guess what comes next. It's giving me whiplash to try.

So, after he takes my cup and sets it back, when he turns, still naked, and whispers, "Scoot over," I listen. I shuffle backward on the queen mattress and lay down on my side so I can watch him.

He gets into the bed right next to me and throws his arm over me, holding me close. Cuddling me. Drawing one of my legs over his waist and drawing soft circles on my hip. We spend a long moment just staring into one another's eyes and

I try to absorb the fact that this is actually real. We're actually here together. When I woke up this morning, I never thought we would get to have a moment like this. I didn't believe it was possible.

I don't know if reality has sunken in, but whatever this dazed, lazy feeling—like floating on my back in a lake with the summer sun warming me up—is, I'm here for it.

After a minute or so, Gunnar whispers, "I need to stretch you, baby."

We're not done? I'd just cooled down to a low, rolling simmer, but when his hand slides down from my hip to my inner thigh, I heat right back up.

I'm still fully dressed in my pajamas, and I open my mouth, about to say something about it, when he orders, "Stand up and strip for Daddy."

"Yes, sir."

I slide my legs off the side of the bed and stand up near the window. I take a step back so that the dull light from outside is on me—so he can see me better. Even though I feel self-conscious, I really, really want to give him what he wants. A show.

Luckily, Gunnar doesn't want a professional. He wants simple, otherwise there's no way he'd want me. *I can do what he wants,* I tell myself, even though goosebumps rise on my arms.

Instead of focusing on what I'm doing as I slide my sleep shorts off, I concentrate on his eyes. I try not to think about myself so I don't become self-conscious. I try to think about my effect on him. And if his eyes are any indication, I'm a fucking goddess. They're burning into me right now, his gaze full of fiery worship. As his eyes scan up and down my frame and he fists my sheet, I feel a surge of power at the fact that he has to restrain himself. That he wants to see me naked so badly. That power gives me the confidence to slowly tease my shirt up my torso before whipping it off over my head and throwing it at him.

He doesn't bother trying to catch it. I'm not wearing a bra and his eyes fix on my breasts as I lower my arms. My nipples tighten and a little rush of delightful friction skitters down my spine. I *really* like the way he's staring.

"So hot, baby. You're so hot. Take those panties off for me now. Let me see all of you."

I slide my panties down my legs, losing that eye contact that's kept me going. I bite my lip as I straighten back up, nerves making me tense until he groans. When I glance up, I can see his hand is on his dick, which is slowly coming back to life—far sooner than I would have expected.

He strokes himself gently as he says, "Touch yourself for me. Let me see what you like."

I reach down and slowly drag my fingers through my trimmed hair, wondering if he minds that I'm not completely bare. I'm soaked, my labia still swollen from earlier, and a few slow passes make me catch my breath. Then I start to circle the way I love.

"Spread your legs. I want to see more."

I slowly part my legs, and use my fingers to widen my slit, sliding up and down as shivers coast through my body.

After a minute, Gunnar's low command rumbles through the room. "Come here."

Eagerly, I drop my hand and move for the bed. I lie down on my side facing him only for him to roll me onto my back and climb on top of me.

Immediately, his weight presses me deliciously into the mattress in a way that makes me feel trapped and caged in. I couldn't stop whatever comes next if I tried. That knowledge sends a surprising thrill through me. I want him to hold me down and own my body.

"You make me crazy." I've never wanted anyone to pin me down before. Of course, anyone else wouldn't be him.

"Same, baby. So much the same it hurts." He begins gently planting innocent kisses on my lips. "First, I'm going to kiss you. Everywhere."

"I like that plan."

He chuckles against my skin, leaving a warm tickling sensation behind. "I thought you would."

His lips leave mine and he drags them over my neck, his rough five o'clock shadow brushing over my delicate skin as he sucks at my pulse. I twine my fingers into his hair as he kisses along my collarbone and then blows a warm trail across my breast until he comes to my right nipple. When he takes it into his mouth, I can't help but gasp.

So good. Especially when his other hand comes down to play with me, the callouses from weight-lifting rasping over my nipple before he starts to pinch it.

I let out a whimper and his warm, wet tongue stops playing. "Remember to stay quiet for me."

Right. Yes. That part of the game. I kind of forgot about it. Okay. Quiet. I imagine we're at a hotel. No, a party. We've snuck upstairs to one of the bedrooms and we have to keep quiet so the hosts won't find us ….

Instead of mewling as he tongues my breast, I dig my fingers into his hair. Take note of how hard his body is against mine, how hot his warm length is where it rests heavy on my thigh.

I unlatch a hand from his hair, exploring his massive shoulder, running my fingers down his pecs, across the short trimmed hair there, over a nipple. I do my own playing. I wish I could do more but there's no chance I can reach his cock, not with the way he has me positioned and has slid down my body with his kisses. But I want to touch him. I can't wait to have that kind of control over him again. I want to see that dazed look once more—figure out exactly what it is.

His mouth does something to my nipple that makes me lose focus, his suckling sending steady pulses through my torso that gather in my cunt. I'm half-convinced his plan is to make me come from nipple-play alone when he releases my breast with a pop and he kisses down my belly as his other hand continues tugging at my other nipple, keeping me on the verge of madness. When his mouth reaches my inner thighs, I have to bite my lip. *God, yes.*

His scruff drags along my thighs, the warmth of his breath ghosting over the spot where I need him most. My body recognizes what's happening and thrumming anticipation courses through me. All my focus zeroes in on his touches down there. The warmth of his breath, the scrape of his beard, the light touch of his mouth right at the junction of my thigh and torso.

"Daddy!" I beg. I can't get any other words out.

The hand not manipulating my breast comes down and I can feel him pull me apart. He pauses to stare down at me. Into me.

"So pretty," he murmurs before diving in. The flat of his tongue licks up my length and I swear I've never felt anything so amazing. That is, until he blades his tongue and licks up and down each side of my slit.

It's impossible to stay quiet. Impossible not to moan. And when his mouth closes over my clit and he sucks hard, a tidal wave of heat washes over me. It feels so good that I can hardly breathe. He starts up a rhythm and that heat surges through me, sweeping away all my thoughts, all but one.

More.

He works my body perfectly, tugging my nipple, using his mouth, and then letting his other hand slowly slip inside. First, he just uses the tip of one finger, exploring me, lightly thrusting. My body is so ready for him, I think he's surprised at how easily he slides inside.

His eyes fly up to meet mine, but I have nothing more than a lust-drunk expression to offer him. My insides are sparkling and when he gently adds a second finger, stretching me, I can only groan. I've used two fingers on myself before, but his fingers are just so much bigger. I have a dildo … but compared to his dick … I think this is going to be a whole new experience. I can feel his fingers sliding, then scissoring lightly, and the sensation is intense.

"Careful," I warn, reminding him to be gentle. "You might break me."

"If you need your safe word, use it."

"And lose out on an orgasm? Yeah, no thanks."

He chuckles. "Then you might need to take a tiny bit of pain with your pleasure, baby."

He says that, but his motions contrast his words. His fingers slow, giving me time to adjust while he increases the suction. I lose focus on my worries because hot tingles rush up my spine, and my entire body vibrates with need. I yank on his hair, writhing against his face as I chase my pleasure. He speeds back up, possibly even adding another finger. I'm beyond knowing things at this point.

Stars spin behind my eyes, transforming into streaks of pure energy. My legs find their way up to wrap around Gunnar's torso. He doesn't let up, not even when I dig my heels into the middle of his back and use them for leverage to lift my hips and fuck his face.

"GOD YES!" I scream, past any and all playing as the world tumbles down around me and an orgasm rips me to bits.

I writhe and spasm jerkily against him, and his fingers pummel me harder and I can feel myself clenching down on them, feeling so full, so right … until the sensation becomes too much.

"Stop," I whimper, and he immediately pulls his hand from my breast and his lips rise up from my swollen clit, eyes dancing as he turns to look at me.

He watches me as I catch my breath and my feet and hands start tingling. "You made my limbs fall asleep!" I accuse.

He only smirks at me. "That's because your body knew it needed blood in other places. Now, look down here. I want you to watch, baby. Watch my fingers come out of you. Look how wet you just got for me."

He leans back then, so I can see. Both of us stare down at his hand as he slowly extracts two fingers from inside me. I hiss in post-orgasm sensitivity but when his fingers are free, I can't help but stare. They're absolutely drenched. Phantom tingles roll through me when he brings them both to his mouth and sucks.

I don't expect it when he falls forward on the bed, planting his hands on either side of my shoulders so that he makes me bounce slightly underneath him as he ends up in missionary position.

I giggle and smack at his chest, which ends up with me gliding my fingers through his trimmed chest hair as he smiles down at me softly.

"You're so pretty when you laugh, Daise," he whispers. And my heart melts.

I've never felt like this before ... but right now, I'm engulfed in a warm sensation, like I'm swimming through sunshine.

I think it might be love.

It's definitely not just lust for Gunnar. I've felt that for ages. It's not friendship either—we've been able to tease and rile each other up since the moment we met. This is different. Right now, I feel this soft sort of tenderness too. I bring my hand up to cup the side of his face, the rough texture of his five o'clock shadow prickling against my palm. I can't believe that out of all the people in the world he actually wants me.

My eyes start to mist and he grumbles, "No crying. Or Daddy will think you don't like what he did and won't do it again."

I laugh through my tears. "Don't make threats you don't intend to keep, old man."

"Old man!" He thrusts his length up against my sopping sex and I can feel how hard he is. "Does that feel like an old man's dick to you?"

"Dunno. I haven't really gotten to feel it yet," I tease, giggling and blinking until the annoying droplets smear down my cheeks and I can swipe them away.

"Oh, you're gonna feel it. Just for that, I'm not going to go as slow as I planned."

"Considering how slow you were downstairs, I'm pretty excited about that. Not sure I'm ever letting you drive to the grocery store again though. I could probably walk faster—"

"Brat!"

His thrust puts an end to all my sass. With a single shove, Gunnar seats himself inside my channel and I have to suck in a breath. It's so fucking intense—far bigger than his fingers. He doesn't press in all the way, just hovers with about four inches inside of me, sliding back and forth gently.

"What were you complaining about, baby girl? I couldn't hear you."

I don't have any smart retorts left. All I can do is clamp my hands down on Gunnar's triceps as he sets up a rhythm and starts to ride me. It hurts at first, in a sharp, pinching way. But as he continues, slow and steady for who knows how long because time starts to lose its meaning, the pain starts to ease, and I can breathe again.

He knows immediately when that happens. I must relax my limbs or something, because suddenly he's dipping down and stealing a quick kiss.

"Better?"

I nod.

Then he lowers his arms, wrapping them around my back, hugging my body to his as he strokes in and out of me, a tiny bit deeper than before. "It's going to be okay, baby. I'm going to take care of you."

His hands slide down to my lower back and grab my ass. The spots he spanked earlier squeal in pain, but he lifts my butt and it changes the way his dick hits inside of me.

Instead of stroking deep, he thrusts shallowly and the thick mushroom head of his cock taps against … something. *Fuck! What is that?*

"It's so intense," I whine, writhing, trying to get away.

But Gunnar holds me in place and keeps going. "Trust me, baby. You're going to like it."

"It's too much!" I argue.

"Daisy, are you going to use your safe word? Or are you going to submit?"

That makes me clamp my lips together. I study his eyes and he stops for a moment, awaiting my decision.

"Promise it will feel better." I beg, because I need to know.

He dives down and kisses me, sucking on my lower lip for a moment before releasing it. "Promise," he whispers, his lips moving across my own as he makes that vow.

And I believe him. Wholeheartedly and completely. Because Gunnar has never let me down. I reach up and stroke his cheeks as I nod, giving him my consent, my trust, my submission.

"Wrap your legs around me," he commands.

I do what he asks, and he shifts slightly, creating more space between our torsos. "Now, put your hand between us and finger that clit."

"It's already too–"

"Daisy, I don't want to spank you right now, baby. But I will. I'll flip you over doggie style and spank you as I fuck you."

That mental image ties together with the sensations floating through my body and I end up writhing underneath him.

"Hand," he orders.

This time, I don't hesitate to obey, because I can feel my body climbing up that invisible hill, nearing the peak. Whatever he's doing … it's working. It's like my body is adjusting to the intensity of that sensation, and instead of wanting less, now I want more.

I don't bother telling Gunnar that he's right. The bossy fucker knows it anyway. I put my thumb and forefinger on either side of my clit and tug.

"Good girl," he praises and he gradually starts to fuck me harder, eventually working up to a pace that makes his thick balls slam into my ass and add another layer of sensation.

This is what it's like to be fucked, used, ridden. It's nothing like what I expected from all the porn videos. Watching can't describe the way his dick spreads my sensitive lips, the slide against them making me instinctively want to swivel and grind, not just take it like the girls on TV do in order to give the camera the best angle. Dirty books don't even get it right. They always describe mind-numbing after-effects … but not the mind-blanking, animalistic need that comes right before.

All I can think about is coming. Hard.

"Baby, let me hear you," Gunnar says as he fucks me so forcefully I slide up on the pillow, my head precariously close to the headboard.

"But, Daddy, I don't want to get caught by the other people at the party," I breathe. "If they find us, we'll get kicked out."

That sends him over the edge. "Oh God." He ruts me with wild abandon, words flying from his mouth. I only catch half of them because I'm too busy tugging at my clit with one hand and shoving the other above my head to brace myself so I don't smash into the headboard from his thrusts. The words I do catch are "perfect," "hot," and "Daddy's pussy."

Oh God, yes. "It's your pussy. Yours."

He grunts and his fingers dig into my ass as he comes, which is the most exquisite torture, because I swear, his dick gets even warmer inside of me as he does. Tugging my clit hard, I follow almost immediately after, and I'm surprised by how much more satisfying it is to clench down on a thick, hard dick than on a pair of fingers. It's bliss … pure, unrivaled, mindlessness. I swivel my hips, drawing out the sensation, his cock twitching deliciously inside of me as a result. His back tenses underneath my heels, but I don't let up. He got his orgasm, and I'm getting mine. I writhe up into him again.

He gives a gasp and that delicious little surge of sensual power I felt before when he watched me with burning eyes returns two-fold. *That's right, Gunnar. You might be my daddy, and I might be your sub. But I own you.* I milk every bit of my own orgasm out of his dick.

After the last strings of my pleasure unwind, I release him from the death grip of my thighs, dropping my feet and letting myself sink into the mattress.

Gunnar plants an exhausted kiss on my pulse before carefully pulling out of me and rolling over to my side.

I stare at the ceiling in a dull, spent way—my thoughts fuzzy like I haven't gotten enough sleep. Excellent orgasms will do that to a girl, apparently. I just never knew before. But now I do.

There's an ache between my thighs I haven't felt before, but it's not unpleasant … it's kind of a satisfying reminder of what just happened.

My head turns on the pillow to look over at Gunnar. His shower's been completely wasted because a thin sheen of sweat plasters his hair to his forehead. He blinks up at the ceiling, looking just as out of it as I feel. My heart lifts because I've never seen him look more disheveled. Or more perfect.

GUNNAR

est sex of my life. No doubt about it. One piece of my mind is lazily congratulating me, still riding the orgasm high, still reveling over how perfectly tight Daisy was, and the way her lush mouth popped open at the end when I fucked her good and deep. And that's just the physical side of things.

I don't even know how to process the emotional connection I felt yet. It's not even just the overwhelming craving for her, the pent-up explosion of desire after waiting for so long.

There was just a rightness to being with her. The way she looked up at me with adoration and complete trust after I promised her it would feel better. No one has *ever* looked at me that way before—and that look is worth more than gold.

Precious.

She's completely and utterly precious.

Most of my life, I haven't prioritized emotions. I've always thought the people who did were fools. Order, structure, science—those things made sense. Now, I finally realize what they're talking about--how being with the right person can be this soul-deep experience. I'm a religious skeptic, but for a moment there ... we touched on something ethereal. Some gauzy, light-filled plane of existence I've never been to before.

Magic. That's the closest I can come to describing it.

Even as I have that emotional revelation, the logical side of my brain is already cracking the whip. *You were way too damn hard on her for her first time, you selfish bastard. And after the screw up with the spanking you aren't allowed any more mistakes. After care, right fucking now.*

That side is right. Like always. Even prepping her probably wasn't enough. She's probably sore as shit. I need to erase that pain and take care of her. I shove myself up to a sitting position, though my body would rather just close its eyes and nod off. Too bad. My body learned long ago during residency that it's not in charge though, so when I get to my feet, it shoves a little adrenaline my way, resigned to the fact that its needs will be shoved aside until they're convenient.

Daisy immediately clears her throat and her voice is soft as she asks, "Are you leaving?" I turn to look down at her and see her pressing her lips tightly together.

"Just getting you some things to clean up and help make sure you're not hurting later."

"Oh." The anxiety on her sweet face immediately recedes and her cheeks relax into an embarrassed smile. "You don't have to—"

I hold up a hand to cut her off. "Yes, I do. I want to take care of you."

Her face relaxes into an expression I can't quite name. It's a kind of soft gratitude mixed with devotion—I love that look, and I definitely want to prove myself worthy of it.

I gather supplies and return to see Daisy emerging from the bathroom. Perfect.

"Lay down and spread your legs."

Her hands come protectively in front of herself, shyness overtaking her once more.

I shake my head as I lay out my items on the bedside table. Then I walk around to her. Taking her face in my hands, I cup it and run my thumbs in gentle circles over her cheeks. I wait until her eyelashes are fluttering before I lean down and give her a soft kiss. She melts, just like I want her to. That's when I whisper, "That's Daddy's pussy, baby, remember? Mine. I need to take care of it."

She lets me lead her over to the bed and I don't miss the wince when she climbs up. Dammit. She chews her lip as she hesitantly lies down on her back, those blue eyes of hers bright pools in the dark room as she watches me sit on the edge beside her. Gently, I pry her legs apart. Then I reach for the warm wet rag in a bowl that I brought from the other bathroom. Squeezing out the excess water, I wipe her down. I'm careful not to press hard or swipe too much, letting the heat soothe her more than anything.

"Um … we forgot to use a condom," Daisy's face turns bright red as she realizes that fact.

"No we didn't," I reply flatly, focused on my job.

"But …"

"I got snipped years ago. So don't worry."

"Oh," She immediately breathes out a sigh of relief. "You did. Why?"

"Not really the fatherly type." I shrug.

"You're the Daddy type," she quips and I grin down at her.

"Yes. That I am. But I'm so glad I did it because it means I got to feel you. So soft and tight and warm, baby. It felt so good. And the way you submitted? You made me so happy."

Her lips press together in a shy smile at the praise. I make a mental note to give her more of it. Because as much as I adore sparring with her bratty side, this soft complacency absolutely destroys me.

"I liked submitting," she admits.

"Thank goodness."

"Right? Who knew we'd be so perfect for each other?"

I just smile down at her. I did. I knew from the moment I met her. I take a deep breath, not ready to tell her, scare her. If she can still accidentally say yes to dates with other guys we are definitely not on the same page of obsession yet.

One day.

I hope.

"How sore are you?" I ask, studying her sweet face, still disbelieving that I'm here in her room, buck naked beside her. The universe has never been this kind to me before, and my natural suspicion is roused for a moment, before I douse it. I will not look this gift horse in the mouth.

"I'm fine," Daisy replies in one of those bright voices my patients put on when they're lying through their teeth.

My jaw stiffens. I turn to the nightstand where I laid out other supplies. "Here. Take a Tylenol. And no lying, honey. I don't want to make that a rule, but I have to trust you and you have to trust me."

I stare at her long enough to ensure she gets the message. Once she gives a small nod, I hand her the pill and a glass of water before I put the rag on my thigh and grab a bottle of lube I brought.

"No, please. I'm done. I'm so, so done." She tries weakly to wave me off.

"Shh … I'm just going to put a little on you. A little lube after a hard session will make the skin down there less sensitive." I gently bring my lubed fingers to her crotch, careful not to directly touch her skin as I smooth it on.

She hisses anyway. "It's cold."

"Sorry. But I think you'd kill me right now if I tried the warming lube."

She chuckles her agreement and sighs as I finish. "Thanks. That does feel a little better."

"Almost done," I tell her. Naturally, some of the lube clings to her little patch of pubic hair, so I use the rag to dab at the excess before standing up and walking to her bathroom to toss the rag into the sink.

"You know what?" she calls out as I turn to walk back.

"What?"

"Your ass looks even better naked."

I chuckle as she yanks a sheet up over herself, arranging her blankets, trying to pretend she's nonchalant instead of blushing furiously after her admission.

"So you were looking at my ass before this?" I query.

"Who wouldn't?"

"True," I give her a satisfied smile and a wink as I pull a corner of the quilt back and slide in beside her.

She blinks up at me, those long lashes slightly clumped together after the tears she shed earlier. "You're staying?" Her voice is small and hopeful.

"If you want me to," I tell her.

"Always," she grins bashfully, her face so cute, the apples of her cheeks drawing my hands like magnets.

Always. She can't possibly mean it literally, but that doesn't matter. I take it that way. Because I want to. Because the monster inside of me needs to. I'm *always* going to stay at her side.

* * *

DAISY SLEEPS PEACEFULLY through the night. I don't. After an hour, I'm sitting up in her bed, staring down at her.

Her hair is a messy tangle, her lips softly parted, her hands tucked underneath her cheek. Adorable.

How many times have I watched her like this? Dreamed about this? And now she's here, naked in front of me. Now she's actually mine.

The sick, twisted part of me wants to yank her out of bed right now and force her to her knees, making her blow me again, not because I'm already hard—just because I can. Because she agreed to be my sub. Because she said yes.

But that darker part of me is overshadowed for the first time in a long time by this tender, content knowledge: Daisy belongs to me.

It's still a surreal fact that floats through my head like a dandelion seed—impossible to catch and hold onto.

I try to appease the demon whispering in my ear by thinking, *One day. One day, we'll hold her down as we fuck her face until she's choking* ... God, my fantasies have warped in the year and a half I've spent pining after her, feeding this dominant daddy fantasy until it's this massive, nearly unmanageable beast.

Right now, I'm ahead. Right now, she's doing really well submitting to my rules, playing along with my kinks. There's no way I'll fuck this up or let my control slide into something darker and more depraved. No way.

For a while, I imagine how good she's going to look on my arm at those stupid work dinners I hate. The holiday party. She'll be so beautiful that those things might just become tolerable. Showing her off as mine might even make me enjoy them.

Of course, that will be after everyone swallows their judgment.

If my co-workers thought me marrying a patient was scandalous, what would they think when they find out I'm dating that woman's daughter? My own stepdaughter? Those imaginary work dinners warp into nightmare images where everyone is glaring at us and making her uncomfortable and me angry.

Maybe we should keep things low-key for a bit. Let ourselves get used to this thing first. Yes, that sounds like a good plan.

So, instead of Christmas parties, I imagine us on a tropical vacation where nobody knows us or will judge us, in a private villa with its own pool and Daisy is skinny dipping, emerging from the pool with water cascading down her body.

Much better.

We've made so many nice, PG-rated memories already. I need to make so many more naughty ones.

I wonder what she'll do when I try to play with her in public —finger-fucking her in a movie theater and ordering her to be quiet. Will she be able to last? Keep quiet and still when we really do have an audience and could get kicked out?

What about when we go to a restaurant? I gaze down at Daisy right now. She's curled onto her side, breathing evenly, the pert line of her nose and then the column of her neck drawing my eyes. Will my girl slide under the table so she can suck my cock when I tell her to?

What about when I add another layer of danger by inviting her friends ... taking them all to a club, getting them drunk, sending the others off to dance, and then forcing Daisy to walk to the bathroom and take off her panties, to sit next to me and spread her legs, trying to keep her face passive while I whisper in her ear and pinch her clit ... telling her she should invite one of the girls home to play ... I wouldn't let her. It would ruin the perfect trust between us and I don't want anyone but her. But I'd want her to get up, start to walk away, be willing to ask. Be willing to do anything for me, just like I would for her.

I don't want to push her too far ... but I do want to push. And push. Until those limits of hers expand little by little.

God, if I hadn't come twice tonight already, I'd be hard as a rock right now. As it is, I'm halfway there, but age is catching up with me. Which is exactly why I don't want to waste a minute now that I've got my girl. My one and only.

I slide out of bed, careful not to jostle her before padding down the hall to my room naked, I grab my cell phone from the charger and wander into my closet to slide on a robe.

Reading glasses. Where did I put those damn things? I find them on my dresser and toss them on before I type out a quick text to work, telling them I've come down with something. There's zero chance I'm going in tomorrow.

I'm going to revel in this newfound thing between us.

But she has a test coming up so she can't just play hooky all day.

Dammit.

I haven't followed Daisy for a while ... not like I used to. I used to watch from my bedroom window whenever she went swimming in the backyard, long legs kicking as she swam laps.

A couple of times, I followed her to the movies, telling myself I just wanted to ensure she was safe—that she wasn't lying and going to some rave or something. But then, somehow, I ended up in the back of the same theater ... just watching her. Just staring at her profile, ignoring the screen when any jokes came along, just so I could see her laugh.

Maybe I should do that tomorrow. I mean, now that she knows, it's different, the guilt won't trail after me as I follow her. It will be better. Mmm … yes. I make my way back to my girl's bed, plans for the next day taking shape.

Very improper plans.

* * *

WHEN DAISY FINALLY WAKES, I've done my morning workout routine, had two cups of coffee, gotten a special delivery, and made breakfast. Shirtless, so my girl can enjoy the view.

"Hey, sleepyhead," I come around the counter to greet Daisy as she shuffles into the kitchen, a warm robe thrown on to cover her up and keep away the morning chill. Even though the weather's been pleasant during the day lately, nights get down in the thirties or so. She's rubbing at her eyes and yawning when I reach her.

I plant a kiss on the top of her head and she looks up at me with furrowed brows, a look that could be pain or confusion.

"Need another Tylenol?" I ask softly, taking her hand and leading her to the kitchen table so she doesn't have to climb up onto a counter stool when she's sore.

"Yes, please," she blushes as she sits.

I get her medicine, coffee, and the plate of pancakes and eggs I made for her. "Here, eat up. I'm going to go lay out your clothes for the day."

Her head jerks up at that.

I expected it, so I grin. "It won't be every day, but some days … Daddy's going to dress you. Okay?"

She presses her lips together and nods, giving me neither the heated glance nor the sassy retort I was prepared for. Instead her expression droops, resembling the sad melancholy she fell into when Darla passed.

"What is it?" I stop where I am, studying her face, panic rushing through me as my mind races, wondering what I might have done to upset her.

"Is … what we did … it is wrong? Would she—"

I march over, determined to nip this in the bud. I pull out the wooden chair next to her and sit down on it sideways so that I'm facing her instead of the table. Putting a hand gently on the knee that protrudes from her robe, I say, "Daisy. We're taking care of each other. We're just two people who are drawn to each other. That's all." I trace little circles on her knee, trying to soothe her with touch.

She shakes her head, not quite convinced. "But–"

"You deserve happiness too. Especially after … as far as I'm concerned, the universe owes you like ten years of happiness after everything you went through. She'd want you to be happy, baby. Us to be happy." My words are soft and gentle, but I hope the truth of them pierces my girl like an arrow. Because Darla would never stand in the way of anything Daisy wanted.

After a moment, a soft admission spills from her lips. "I always wondered, selfishly, why you didn't ask me out instead."

"Because how could I ask you to give me a broken heart? You needed to heal first."

"You didn't have to marry her for that." She ducks her head, probably embarrassed of the jealousy that spilled out in her tone. But I love it.

I reach out and take her chin in my hand, lifting her face until our gazes meet. "You also needed more time with her. Marrying her ... it made it possible for me to get insurance, ask for favors, get what was needed ... buy you that time."

Tears fill her eyes and she doesn't even try to bat them away. I wipe them for her with gentle brushes of my thumbs.

"Things work out the way they're supposed to," I whisper, before leaning down and giving her a soft kiss.

"I kind of think so too," she agrees.

I pull her into a hug, not all the way into my lap, but as close as we can get. I hold her until her breathing calms and she pushes lightly on my chest. "Okay. Okay. You're suffocating me with all your chest hair."

"You love my chest hair."

She giggles and it does my heart good to hear it. I know we'll probably have this same conversation dozens of times because guilt isn't nice and logical—I've struggled with my own over the past year and a half and am well versed in how it can play on an endless loop. But we'll get through this together.

I stand up, studying her face, ensuring her expression is clear. Then I let my dominant side slip forward. "Now, eat your breakfast, then come to your room."

"Yes, sir," she mocks, back to her sassy self. Yeah. She's good.

"I might go easy on your sore pussy today, honey, but make no mistake, I will still spank your ass."

She waits until I'm in the hall before calling out after me. "Promises, promises!"

I grin and shake my head as I go into her room. Little brat. I hope she never changes.

Forty minutes later, Daisy's showered, her hair is dried and done, and she's wearing a blue sweater dress that makes her eyes pop, thick socks, and a bra. No panties. We're arguing over the little scrap of lace she holds in her hands.

"It's going to be uncomfortable. And, what if it just slides down, huh?" she grumbles as she eyes the black garter belt in her palm.

"Your job is to make sure that doesn't happen. No one should see that garter."

"Then why am I wearing it?" she asks in frustration. "Especially to school."

I take a step forward, putting my hand on her neck and sliding it around back. I bend forward and watch as her eyelids flutter shut. Only a day, and she's already expecting me to kiss her.

I reward that reaction, planting a soft peck on those lips. I crave more, but now isn't the time. So I lift up slightly and let my whisper caress her mouth instead. "I want you to think of me with every step you take. Every time you sit down, that lace will brush your inner thighs and make you remember me. Daddy wants you to walk around, clamping that skirt down around those legs so that no one else gets to see what's his."

"Oh, fuck. Fuck."

"Daisy …" I straighten, biting down on a smile when she naturally tries to follow, leaning toward me as those bright blue eyes pop open, entranced.

"Yes?" she whispers.

"Two swears. Five bucks for the swear jar."

"But …"

"If Daddy isn't plowing his cock into your little pussy, then you don't get to say fuck."

I turn and stride out of the room, already digging into my pocket as she yells after me in a ragged, breathless voice, "Seven-fifty."

I yank out a ten and wave it in the air. "Worth it."

"Evil!" she calls out.

She has no idea.

In the hall, I turn back, only to see her yanking the garter up her shapely leg. *God. Next time I need to bite those thighs and mark them.* I shift my dick in my pants and then go pretend to get ready for work.

I have some stalking to do.

* * *

I SENT her off with my phone and told her I'll bring her new phone to her later even though I already have the new one. I paid a king's ransom for mid-morning delivery … I just want an excuse to see her later because I know there's no way I'll be able to wait until tonight.

I drive down to the university and fight for parking, flipping off some floppy-haired stoner when I slide into the spot he wanted. I open up Daisy's new phone and click the tracking app I downloaded so I can find her.

I walk through the campus, weaving around the many adobe-style buildings, a brisk wind blowing in from the east tugging at my hair. The weather makes me grin because it will make it even harder for Daisy to follow my rule as she walks between classes.

I need to find a spot where I can observe that delicious struggle and make sure she's being a good girl.

I walk past the duck pond, which is empty of ducks at the moment. The water is a dull brownish-gray, even though the sky is clear today. The water is as suspicious as I am, lurking under the shade of a tree, watching students spill out the doors of their classes.

They're so fricking young. I remember what I was like back then, all brash and arrogant. Daisy would probably say nothing's changed about me. But she'd be wrong. Back then, I had no patience. Now, I've learned to appreciate the glorious thrill of taking things slow.

I glance at the phone and see her dot moving. Then I glance up to watch her push through the turquoise double doors of a building, emerging from it. She immediately cringes when she feels the whip of the wind. Her fingertips fly down to her hemline, making me grin.

Good girl.

Scurrying down a twisting sidewalk, she walks alone, hands clutching her dress carefully.

I notice a guy watching her from behind. *Is that the little fucker who asked her out?*

He ducks off and heads the other direction, so maybe not, but jealousy heats my blood anyway.

Maybe this was a bad idea, pushing her to come to class … to move forward with things. Those little punks will be sniffing around her like dogs.

I grind my teeth as I turn to follow her, arguing internally with myself over the fact that she needs to pass her class versus the fact that I need to ensure she knows who owns her—body and soul. She turns a corner, some stupid juniper bushes hiding her from view, and I quicken my steps, heart thudding faster.

There she is, going up the stairs to a humanities building, hurrying even though I'm pretty certain her next one starts on the hour. She has ten whole minutes left.

What I could do to her in ten minutes.

I find myself hurtling up the stairs behind her, bumping into several students without offering any apology. *Where is she?* My eyes scan the corridors, but my girl has already disappeared.

I yank her new phone from my pocket. I'm going to text her. It's the same number as her old one, so she'll easily recognize the call.

But that's when I see a new message on her screen from a contact labeled only Justin—no last name. Her phone never buzzed because I set it to silent, not wanting a barrage of her Wild Flower group texts annoying me all morning.

I click to open the message and read: *Hey! Just wanted to make sure we're still on for tomorrow night. Looking forward to seeing you.*

Lava rips through my chest and for a moment I burn, unable to see anything around me. But I breathe deeply and slowly, until gradually, it cools and hardens into resolve.

I know just what to do.

I text back to that little fucker: *Great, see you then.*

Then I stride down the hall, checking classrooms. If I yank open the door to an occupied one, I just give a curt, "Sorry, wrong room," and move on.

Finally, I find an open one.

Classroom 118 is empty, it even has some desks piled up in the corner that make it look like storage. Perfect. That means we won't get interrupted.

I yank Daisy's phone out of my pocket again and text my own number. *Come to classroom 118 now. Daddy needs to see you.*

Patience gone, blood racing, jealousy fueling me … It's definitely time to remind my Daisy just who she belongs to.

GUNNAR

*D*aisy arrives a flustered mess, shoving her dark silky hair behind her shoulders as she scurries into the empty classroom. She stops short when she sees me standing inside with the lights still off, desks and chairs piled behind me marking this room as more of a storage room than one currently in use.

I watch, amused, as she realizes my intentions, which are probably as obvious as my cock tenting my pants right now.

Her eyes widen and she glances behind her—like she's worried someone saw her going into this abandoned class-room and followed her.

The only person following you is me, baby.

When she turns toward me, her breathing is shallow. I can't tell if those little nipples of hers are peaked beneath her sweater dress, but I'm betting so.

Just her presence makes me dizzy with lust and I wonder if she feels the same. Overwhelmed.

But there's more than just lust brewing here. As I look down at her, eyes tracing the curve of her glossy lips, I'm struck by a combination of fierce longing and pure awe. Life has put my girl through the wringer. And yet, here she stands, smiling tentatively up at me.

"Hey! That was fast. Dropping off my phone?"

My mind isn't processing her mundane words. It's too busy still trying to digest the reality that she's mine.

I sort of knew it last night. I stayed up. Couldn't sleep. But the beast was in charge then, the filthy part of me laying out plans for her.

Right now, staring at Daisy in her conservative little dress, noting the freckles dotted on her nose, even how the cadence of her voice has normalized—instead of holding that sad, somber note that clung to it the past few months—I can't help but get caught up in the moment.

God, I love this girl.

I don't bother with a greeting. I just meet her eyes and walk toward her, every stride radiating what I feel—this intense reverence edged with obsession.

She skitters backward, toward the door, protesting weakly. "I have class. I'll be late."

"Yes, you will," I mutter, pinning her to the wall next to the door, each of my hands bracketing her head as I lean down over her. I can't resist.

Why did I even let her come to school today?

I want to bask in this feeling, keep us in a little bubble, draw out this honeymoon period of ecstasy.

The only reason my Daisy's going to go back to that class later is to get her things.

I don't bother to lock the door, though I easily could. Part of me likes tempting fate that way. *Maybe some student will even walk by and assume a professor is getting his extra credit served up. Mmm. I like that thought.* Maybe that's a game I'll add to my fantasy wishlist, which is already so damn long I'm pretty sure it rivals Santa's.

I lean down and inhale the citrusy scent of her shampoo as I whisper, "Daisy, Daddy needs a kiss. Will you give me one?"

Her lips part and I watch with delight as her eyes dilate while she stares up at me. I stay where I am, looming over her, waiting to see what she'll do. Her tongue darts out and swipes at her lower lip before she extends up on her tiptoes towards me.

I let her initiate since I asked for it, keeping my lips gentle against hers, letting her be the aggressor as the kiss deepens. I tease her by pulling my chin back and making her chase after me, until she's giggling adorably and whispering, "Stay still."

God, she does things to me.

I could keep this encounter innocent. I should. We're on campus, people know her here; I don't want to jeopardize her future. But the demon on my shoulder, the one who's whispered in my ear since the moment I saw her, slips inside my head and takes the reins.

After holding him back for so long, it feels impossible to just give him an inch. He wants it all.

"That was very sweet. But that wasn't the kind of kiss I meant. You kissed the wrong spot," I murmur.

Her scandalized little inhale makes me smile, but other than that, I don't move. My dick has been hard since this morning when I solidified my plans to follow her, and I've resisted touching it … edging myself by waiting for an opportunity. Now, I have one.

Of course, my girl has to go and be a smartass. "Not your mouth, Daddy? Then here?" She dips her head the slightest bit and her lips find my neck, just above my collared shirt. Her teeth come out and nip at me.

"Nope. Not it," I play along. My tone comes out light and bright. But inside of me, a monstrous villain chuckles because Daisy is giving in to corruption. My sweet girl is playing along despite the very heady reality that we're in public and could get caught for real.

"What about *here*?" She bends further and bites down on one of my shirt buttons, pulling back with it clutched in her teeth so she can glance mischievously up at me. Naughty minx.

"You're still cold." I wish I'd set up her phone on an empty desk to record us. I tell my mind to remember this moment forever.

She drops the button. "Am I?" Her brow furrows in mock distress as she sinks to her knees. "What about now?"

My dick twitches in my slacks. God, just the sight of her like that, her dress rising up her thighs, the black garter peeking out from underneath it, the garter she's been trying to hide all day from everyone else.

A tiny bit of precum leaks from my tip at seeing her look so submissive.

I reach down and cup her cheek gently. "Have you figured out where Daddy wants his kiss?"

Her head turns to the side and her lips capture my thumb. She sucks it into her mouth and laves it with her tongue. Popping off the tip, she murmurs, "Your hand, right?"

I swallow a chuckle and pretend to be disappointed. "That's too bad. If you figured out where I wanted my kiss, I was going to give you one in the same spot."

Her tune changes immediately, her amusement morphing to determination as she reaches for my belt. I watch as she carefully undoes it, then moves to the button of my pants. I help her, unzipping them and fishing myself out so that I stay clothed.

But before she can lean forward, I tug on my length and order, "Dress off, baby."

Her look of shock is one for the ages. "But if we get caught …."

"You let Daddy worry about that," I tell her, reaching out and dragging my thumb over the lips that will soon be wrapped around my cock. I'll willingly trade a big chunk of change for a fucking public indecency charge to go away for the chance for my girl to suck me off nearly naked in a classroom. Worth it. "You don't have to worry about anything anymore, princess. I've got you. That's what Daddies are for."

I see her gulp nervously.

I give her a few seconds to come to terms with the idea before I let my tone and face grow crisp in displeasure. "Daisy, you have until the count of five. Otherwise, I'm going to have to get upset."

My balls tighten as her hands go to her skirt and she slowly starts to pull that conservative sweater dress up over her head. I enjoy every single second of that reveal, letting my eyes skim over her perfect form, those round hips and narrow waist. When the dress has been shed, she's left in nothing but an innocent looking bra and that fucking garter. Her brown hair falls gracefully down her back and my gaze traces the delicate curve of her neck, the swells of her breasts, the flat of her tummy, and down to her trimmed snatch.

"Are you wet for me?" I ask.

She nods.

Who knew that it would be this easy? This perfect? That my angel would be so deliciously eager? It's a literal dream come true.

"Good." I step forward, hand on my cock. I place the tip softly against her bottom lip and smear precum over her mouth. "Give me my kiss."

She swallows me down, at least for the first three inches, and sets a quick pace. I don't bother to slow her down because she's nervous, but also because after waiting so long this morning—not even jerking off in the shower—I'm more than ready to feed her my cum. "Oh, you make me feel good, princess. Look at how well you're swallowing Daddy's cock. Can you take a little more?"

She slides down another two inches, nowhere near all the way down, but I can feel myself starting to tap the back of her throat. I don't push, just enjoy it. The little flicks of her tongue, the warm, wet heat of her mouth.

"I can't stop thinking about how sexy you looked last night, naked on your bed for me. You're so beautiful, Daisy. I can't get you out of my head. I'm so proud of how you took my cock. Even when it hurt. You're such a brave girl for Daddy, baby. So good."

My girl responds to my praise by adding that tongue to the mix. Her hand comes up to cup my balls through my pants and a thrill shoots up my spine. I glance down and let my eyes zero in on the shape of her breasts, so soft and round.

"Good job, baby. " I bring my hand to her cheek and slowly pause her.

She leans back, confused, dropping her hands from my shaft and balls. "But, you didn't come."

"I'm about to. Stay still." Her hands fall to her lap and she looks perfect just like that, breath shallow, breasts heaving, lips wet. I glance down at the junction of her thighs, knowing her pussy is probably still sore because of me.

That knowledge does it.

My balls tighten and my lower back heats while my vision tunnels. Quickly, I jack my shaft and aim it at her chest, gritting my teeth as an orgasm rips through me, a wild and feral thing. Ropes of come shoot out to paint her breasts and ruin her bra. I turn my sweet-looking girl into a cum-slut, marking her as mine, masculine satisfaction surging through me at the sight.

"Thank you," I grin down at her.

She simply purses her lips. "You had to do that? How am I supposed to go to class now?"

"You're ditching today."

She grumbles, trying to hide a grin, as she climbs up from her knees, hands gesturing at the delicious lines of cum streaking down her chest. "How am I supposed to clean up?"

"You're not. Daddy wants you dirty." I take a moment to drink in her aggravated expression. "Now go over the teacher's desk while I lock the door. It's time for your kiss."

She presses her lips together, clearly holding back a retort because she doesn't want her turn taken away. Smart girl.

I smirk as I tuck myself back into my pants, redo my belt, and lock the door, which seems unnecessary at this point because the hallway is empty. But I'm guessing it will make my Daisy a little less nervous and distracted.

The dull sound of literary analysis filters through the walls and I cringe. It's not exactly mood-enhancing. But when I see Daisy leaning against the wooden professor's desk, my cum drizzled across her skin, sliding down the valley between her breasts, all that external noise fades away.

I stride over and grab her ass, picking her up with both hands and then setting her squarely in the middle of the desk, her legs spread on either side of my hips. I lift my hands up and slide each of her bra cups down until they're underneath the smooth globes, propping her breasts up for me. Unable to resist the sight of her little nipples, I bend and take one in my mouth, enjoying her delighted little exhale.

I tongue it for a minute, teasing that bud until it's hard before I pull back slightly and lick a line up her chest, gathering up some of the cum I spilled on her. Rising up above her, I grab the back of her neck roughly and pull her in for a punishing kiss, where I feed that cum right back to her. She swallows it down with a naughty little moan, sucking on my tongue, eager for everything I have to give her right now.

God, I'm glad I just came, or I'd be tempted to fuck her and I don't truly want to hurt her.

"Lie back, baby," I order as I release her neck, her hair swaying back behind her. She bites her lower lip as she lies back on the wooden desk using her elbows to prop her up so she can watch. God, the sight of that lace garter on her thigh does things for me. I spread her legs further apart, not because I need to, just because I like the sight of that little gash gaping open for me.

I drag a hand over the breast I didn't touch, tweaking that nipple as I take my time to drink in this moment.

"Daddy, please."

I bend forward, rewarding her for begging so politely by kissing up and down either side of her slit. Just closed mouth kisses first, to tease her. Then short kisses full of darting tongue. Finally, I let my mouth seal over her seam, my tongue sliding out to part it, dip inside and taste her tart flavor, and glide away.

That makes her buck. I end up having to plant my hands on my girl's hips to keep her still. If she's not careful, someone discussing Dante's *Inferno* will wonder what layer of hell is in this room. If they peered through the window in the hall door, they'd discover it was lust.

Pinning Daisy to the desk, I ravish her with my mouth, nuzzling her clit with my nose, the whimpers she makes as I fuck her with my tongue driving me on. Finally, I give her what she needs most, moving my lips up and sealing them over that hot little clit.

I can't stop her bucking then. Even pressing down on her with my shoulders, my Daisy writhes like a woman possessed, her garter dragging back and forth across my cheek. *Fuck yes, baby girl. Come on Daddy's tongue.*

I don't stop, pushing her over the brink again and again. I'm going to teach her to crave the orgasms I give her … until she's as obsessed with me as I am with her.

* * *

"OH MY GOD! STOP!"

Daisy's begging makes me chuckle and I try to shrug her hand off my arm as I continue my victory dance. I just trounced her in Mario Kart.

We're at a brewery—after grabbing her books and ditching her classes we decided to grab a mid-afternoon lunch. This place hardly has anything that can be called food, just cheesy tots and salad slathered in dressing, but my mood is too good to complain much about it. I'll fix us something healthy later. The real benefit of this location is the games available for patrons, games my little flower is apparently horrible at. She's so far lost at corn hole, giant Jenga, and now this.

"I can't stop." I tell her, shaking my hips back and forth as I enjoy the way her hands fly up to cover her face in embarrassment. "This is what winners look like, honey." I ham it up.

"Who are you?" She shakes her head in disbelief and I can't help but grin.

She's right—but I'm fucking giddy as shit right now because being with this girl is better than any drug on the market.

"You should never be allowed to win anything ever again," she declares as she walks away from the giant TV screen on the wall back to our wooden booth, grabbing her iced tea and sucking the straw, deliberately looking away from me.

My smile stretches from ear to ear as I watch her pout. This afternoon has been perfect. Everything has been, like the universe is proving to me how well we go together. Even her annoyance is adorable.

I toss my controller back into the basket set out for them and follow my girl back to our seats, one of only two tables in the whole place that are occupied right now since it's mid-afternoon. Fans whir above us and the sound of a basketball game from a TV screen in the corner drifts over. "You sure I shouldn't? Because I was kind of thinking about the prize I want for winning."

She drops the straw and stares at me suspiciously. "There are no prizes."

"There are always prizes when Daddy's involved, baby." I slide my legs around hers under the table and then slowly close my legs until hers are trapped together and I'm certain she can feel that garter.

"I was thinking my prize could be deciding where I'm going to fuck you next," I tell her.

Her eyes widen and she automatically glances at the other restaurant patrons, though they're at their own wooden booth near the tall windows, wrapped up in their own conversation. Once she's satisfied we're not scandalizing strangers, she turns back to me.

"Do you mean where like a room, or …." She gulps.

I chuckle at her nerves. "Oh sweetheart. Eventually, I'll take you everywhere. But not yet. It's too new for you. Yes, I was thinking like a room." I dig her brand new phone out of my pocket and slide it across the table.

She scoops it up with an excited squeal, but I interrupt her eager delight to set up the new device.

"I'm thinking the campus library would be perfect."

She stops mid swipe. "Wait. What?" Her eyes roam over my face, confused.

I fold my hands on the table and sit back in my seat. "That boy texted you again. And Daddy decided ... you should go on that date."

Her face contorts with what I imagine is disgust mingled with confusion. "But ... why?"

"Because I want to watch you. I want to text you and give you orders. And then I want you to leave his ass and come to me so I can fuck the ever-loving shit out of you."

DAISY

"*W*here were you yesterday?" Rose darts over to me as I stride across campus, hurrying between the theater and the student gym, trying vainly to escape the wind.

Unlike yesterday, where the weather was decent, today, even though the sky is a robin's egg blue, it's deadly cold at nine in the morning. Rose's breath frosts the air as she hugs her gray puffy coat closed and dashes along beside me, doing her best to keep up with my strides even though I'm four inches taller.

I'm grateful for my scarf right now. I hope the orange loop around my neck hides most of my blush as I mumble, "I just spent some time with Gunnar."

Shit. Did I say his name weird? Is she going to notice? I was worried I might slip and say Daddy but now I wonder if my tone of voice is off and that alone gives it away. *God, I should have asked him about what to say to the girls.*

She definitely shoots me an odd look, quirking a brow. "Say what?"

"We just ... went to a brewery and played some games," I explain weakly. "Letting off steam." I rattle off the most innocent of our activities yesterday, even though my mind drifts automatically back to that abandoned classroom and how wanton I felt draped across the top of that desk.

God. That was hot. I very deliberately do not rub my thighs together.

"Your stepfather, Gunnar Strong, Mr. Uptight Extraordinaire —man who has only taken off like two days in his entire life —took off yesterday with you to blow off steam?"

Aw crap. Maybe I should have said Gunnar had a stomach bug instead. I also cringe at the stepfather thing. Couldn't she just see him as a person? Do I bring up the technicality that he's no longer my stepfather or will that just make her suspicious? No. That would definitely let her know something's up.

I give her a lame explanation for our odd behavior. "He knew I needed it, I guess?"

She purses her lips and shakes her head, but luckily, her attention is drawn to Lily—who is striding toward us with mega-freak out energy. Her fur hood is shoved back and her arms are waving her phone in the air as she tries to flag us down. Even though her cheeks are tinged pink with cold, the rest of her face is deathly pale.

"What is it?" Rose asks.

Lily holds out her phone, hand trembling, but the screen has already gone black.

"Um … there's nothing to see," I tell her, pointing at the phone.

"Ugh!" She turns it back to her face to unlock it and Violet comes into view traipsing over the hill where the shuttle bus from the student parking lot lets off.

"Hey," Violet hugs her namesake purple coat around herself as she runs the last few steps to join us. She glances at me, her expression immediately asking "what's up" when she sees Lily grumbling at her phone and then shoving it under Rose's nose.

"See!" Lily says urgently. "He's out!"

Oh, shit.

None of us even have to ask who *he* is. Lily's stalker, Gage Montoya, is the only possible person who could freak her out to this degree. An older guy from Texas, he'd followed her here four years ago. He'd stalked her and videotaped her … and then he'd started emailing her the videos, along with these graphic descriptions of what he wanted to do to her. Not nice things.

Just thinking about it gives me the shivers.

"Hey, hey, you're going to be fine," Rose soothes, running her hand down Lily's back. "I'm sure my mom knows someone who can help." Her mom is campaigning for senator and has pretty much shaken hands with every person in the state.

"If she doesn't, I'm sure my dad does," Violet offers.

Lily's eyes are still filled with tears and she's shaking her head, despite the fact that Violet's offer is as good a guarantee as anything. Her family knows people who could kill this fucker in two seconds flat.

"He's not going to look for you." I try another tactic as I reach for Lily's hand and squeeze. "Look at what happened last time. He got locked up for a good chunk. Repeat offenses are even worse." I shake my head, trying to look confident so that she'll be reassured.

She's not.

"Psychos don't use logic, Daisy," she snaps, pulling away from my hand and leaving the path to pace in the dead grass.

"The unabomber—" I start, but all three of them cut me off with an annoyed look.

"No unabomber!" Violet and Rose declare simultaneously.

I did a project on him for my high school senior year psychology project and they're all basically sick of hearing about him at this point, though it's not my fault he's fascinating. Fucked up. But fascinating.

I smash my lips together and let the other girls take the lead comforting Lily; Violet's far better at that sort of thing than I am. The other girls surround her on either side and start shooting out offers for Lily to come stay with them, to dye her hair, to help her legally change her name … the options mount up as they lead her back onto the path and in the direction of class. I end up trailing behind them.

While I'm willing to do anything to help Lily—while I love her to death—I know how empty a lot of promises can feel when you're facing the thing you fear the most. So I don't offer them up. Instead, I simply meet her eyes when she glances back at me and say, "Anything you need. *Anything.*"

Lily's finally starting to nod at whatever they are saying, a sure sign they're calming her down, when my phone pings with a text.

Can't wait for tonight! Gunnar's text makes a blush immediately bloom on my cheeks. My mind pivots from real world problems to wondering what kind of kinky chaos he's got planned.

It's selfish and immature of me to revel in my own happiness when I know that Lily's worried just ahead, but after living in the dank rot of despair for so long, I cling to this good feeling. To Gunnar and the delicious way he takes control and makes my worries slip away. Even when he does push my limits.

After the garter and the incident in the empty classroom, I have no doubt he's going test them later.

I can't fucking wait.

I wish he would have tested them last night, but he'd simply drawn me a bath and told me I needed to recover before he fucked me senseless again. And of course, he'd reminded me I wasn't allowed to touch myself ... all while he watched me sink down in the water and jerked himself off in front of me, claiming "We're waiting for your own good, but Daddy has needs."

Hot. Fucking. Jerk.

My core heats just recalling the way he stood in the bathroom, steam curling around him. God, he's in such good shape that I'd even traced his thigh muscles with my eyes as he stood wide-legged on the tile, his dick swollen red, tugging faster than I'd ever seen. So fast, I swear it probably hurt. At the end, he grabbed my clean panties from the countertop and came on them, before insisting that I wear them to sleep.

"Your pussy always needs to have a little of my cum on it, baby," he'd said.

God ... his kinks.

Mmmm.

"What are you doing?" Rosie is at my side, peering down at my phone.

I blink back into reality, startled to find we're already at the math building. "Oh, um nothing. Just thinking."

"What does Gunnar mean about tonight?" she asks. "Don't you have your big date?"

Lily and Violet turn back to us, arms linked. Lily's jaw drops. "Ohmygosh! I forgot about the date! How could I? What time do you want us to come over?" Her transition from fear to excitement is a complete one-eighty.

What? Wait. No. I hold up a hand trying to fend off Lily's manic expression. "You don't have to—"

"It will keep my mind off things and get me out of my house, where I'll just be worried he can find me."

"Oh! Maybe we should turn it into a sleepover!" Rose starts clapping her hands, her dark curls blowing across her face.

My mouth drops in horror. No. No-no-no-no. This cannot be happening. My chest grows tight and my stomach drops like I'm riding a roller coaster—but not a good one—one that's utterly terrifying.

I'm not ready for this. I want alone time with Gunnar. I WANT TO GET FUCKED.

I don't want to have to pretend to be good or normal or hide what we are … because I love it. I'm just not ready to share it. "You guys don't have to—"

"It'll be fun! Remember that time we all slept over when Lily went on that date with Kevin Brekker?" Violet grins.

"And I didn't make it back until three in the morning?" Lily laughs.

"Yup," Violet pops her 'p' as she grins. "Then you gave us a full play by play of what went down."

Lily shakes her head with a solemn look. "His dick was so disappointing."

All three of them laugh and I join in, but hollowly. *I mean, how can I refuse to have them over? It's not exactly like I can say, 'Hey girls, so I started fucking Gunnar and I'd like a little bit of privacy—K, thanks, bye.'*

Aloud, I say, "Sounds like so much fun!" Inside, I die a little.

Lily glances over at me. "I'll bring clothes for you."

"Makeup!" Violet calls dibs.

"Why am I always hair?" Rose grumbles, though she knows exactly why. With her natural curls, she's been forced to become a hair expert and can do anything from sleek and straight to even creating those flower rosettes for weddings. She's a hair goddess.

"Guys, isn't this a little overkill? It's just a study date. Like not even a real one," I toss out a weak argument, but I have to try.

They're already pushing through the doors into the building and not a single one of them bothers to respond.

Lily calls out, "Meet at Daisy's at six."

Violet turns to me and orders, "Do not order some health nut salad crap like last time."

And Rose simply blows me a kiss before running back out of the building because her next class is in the building next door.

Fuck. I don't like this. Neither will Gunnar. He's going to be pissed.

* * *

"DAMN, YOU LOOK HOT!" Lily leans back and admires her work after yanking on my shirt to get it to show just the right amount of cleavage.

I don't feel hot. I feel like a nervous wreck. Gunnar's closed himself in his office since the girls showed up. His silent, livid fury from the moment I arrived home until now has my stomach writhing.

He's mad at me. And it's not in a fun way that will get me spanked later.

But what the hell am I supposed to do?

God, I wish Mom was here—though if she was, this never would have happened. Do I wish that? Ohhh, the fact that I'm not sure makes me feel sick to my stomach. Fuck. I shove away the thought of her roughly because if I think too much, I'll just start crying.

Maybe we started this thing too soon. But it feels so right, somehow, like it was inevitable. But then I cycle back to guilt. And the judgment I'm certain I'll see on the faces of my friends. *God, I don't want to think. I just want Gunnar to come up with a solution. To fix it and make it all better, just like he always does. He always takes care of me.* The truth of that realization settles in my bones, because it's true. Before him, I was scrambling, barely keeping my head above water between school, homework, doctor appointments, burnt chicken nuggets, arguments with the insurance company ... He took all that away. Because of him, I started to be able to breathe again. Because of him, I didn't go through everything alone.

Why should I be ashamed to say it out loud? I shouldn't, right? I shouldn't care about their judgment. I should just rip off the Bandaid ....

But I find my tongue stuck to the top of my mouth.

Because even though he healed me, their condemnation would damage that. Mom's loss still aches. And honestly, I'm not ready to hurt again. I'm just not ready.

So I say nothing. I smile wanly into the mirror when Lily spins me around in my desk chair and leans over my shoulder expectantly.

Staring, I hardly recognize myself. I look like someone from social media, some makeup expert, not myself. The Wild Flowers all outdid themselves. My hair is glossy and straight, makeup subtle but sultry with the lashes that Lily applied.

A month or two ago, I might have truly appreciated all their efforts. But now? The eyelashes make me look like I'm trying too hard, it's not the fresh-faced look I'm comfortable in that I know Gunnar likes. I'm also wearing another crop top, this time a peach one with white flowers—which I know he loathes, but all three of them insist this is the in style despite the fact that it's fucking January.

Maybe I can stuff a sweater into my bag and wear it during this joke of a date.

Is Gunnar still going to go now that the girls are interfering? Is he still going to spy on me through the stacks and text me dirty things like he planned? He whispered so many naughty scenarios into my ear last night and I was eager for every damn one of them. Now?

Now, if he's not going, I just kind of want tonight to be over.

I want my friends to go away.

I want the happy little bubble of yesterday back.

"This … is … I don't even recognize myself, girls. You made me look like—"

"A super hot bitch!" Lily toasts herself with a sparkling water that I got delivered along with a huge salad and Dion's delicious, mouthwatering pizza.

"I'm stitching all our clips together into a post," Violet calls out. In the reflection from the mirror, I can see her sprawled on my bed, a folded slice of pepperoni pizza in one hand and her phone in the other. Since her family controls so much of her real life, social media has become her outlet and she's actually pretty damned artistic with her posts.

"Don't put me in any of the shots," Lily quickly states, fear evident on her face.

"Don't worry, nothing but your hands are on here."

I'm about to reassure Lily that Gage isn't going to look for her, but Rose speaks before I get a chance. "It's okay to be nervous about tonight, Daise. It's normal."

Everyone immediately jumps on that reassurance train. "Yeah, getting a few bad dates out of the way is always a good way to get back in the grove," Lily's face smooths out as she stops thinking about Gage finding her and starts worrying about me instead. "Maybe next time, you will even say yes to going to a frat party with Rose and me."

Rose chokes a bit on her pizza, coughing and flailing her hand for a second before saying, "No. *Don't.* Those suck."

"You're just too picky," Lily responds. "But Daisy's not looking to be picky. She needs some practice guys to up her dating game."

I spin back around in my seat and face the room, nodding through all of their advice, though I don't want to be a part of any game unless it's run by the man downstairs.

When my phone pings with a text, it's almost a relief, because I can break eye contact and drop the fake smile that's making my cheeks start to ache.

Come see me before you leave.

My throat dries out. I have no idea what that text means. *Is it good? Is it bad? Is he still furious?* Of course, it's not like he's going to put hearts or anything sweet into a text the girls might see but—

"Why does Gunnar want to see you?" Rose asks, leaning over my shoulder and reading.

"I … maybe to give me one of those lame pre-date lectures?" I have no clue.

"Psh, you're in college. What the hell does he expect?" Lily rolls her eyes.

"My family expects a shit-ton and Gunnar Strong is pretty much on their level of uptight," Violet retorts.

"He's not planning to pick who Daisy marries—so I disagree with you," Lily shoots back.

This conversation is going to make me puke. I stand up in my boots and realize just how queasy I am when I feel dizzy.

"You okay?" Rose's hand comes to my shoulder, rubbing lightly.

I give her a wan grin. "Just nervous. I'm gonna go get this lecture over with."

"Tell him to get fucked!" Violet calls out as I pull open my door.

The girls' giggling fills the room and I close the door on it, leaning back against it for a second and blowing out a breath. Violet has no idea how Gunnar would twist that phrase or how I'd want him to.

The walk down the stairs feels like one of the longest walks of my life, like a space walk, where each step looks like it's in slow-motion. It definitely feels like gravity has left my stomach levitating inside my torso ... I'm so damn nervous.

I knock on the arched wooden door that leads to Gunnar's office and then wait stiffly in the hall until he calls out, "Come in."

I push the door open but keep my eyes downcast, already knowing he's not going to like what he sees. The jean skirt I'm wearing has the kind of rips that showcase the jean pockets and it barely covers my ass.

"Shut it."

I turn and press it closed, ensuring the latch clicks. I don't want the girls overhearing whatever this talk is going to be.

"Lock it."

I twist the lock into place and I swear my stomach shoots out to the side just like that bolt.

When I slowly pivot back to face him, I realize Gunnar's standing behind his desk. Newly published studies are spread out on the surface—he's always reading about break-throughs in this or that. A five o'clock shadow darkens the lower half of his face. When my gaze travels down his arms, I notice he's rolled up his white collared shirt. His forearms flex as he leans over the desk. Flicking my eyes up to his is a mistake, because his look is blacker than midnight.

"Not a fan of that outfit."

His words smack me—even though I was expecting them, I don't think I fully realized how his disapproval would make me want to sink beneath the floor.

"I know," I whisper, casting my eyes down to my feet and toeing the Southwestern area rug.

"No matter what you wear, you're my girl, do you hear me? No one else's."

This time, the fierceness in his tone makes me tingle in delight instead of disappointment.

"Yes, Daddy," I respond, daring to lift my gaze.

God, he looks so good. Huge and strong, with a presence that fills the very room. I want to run to him. But I also want to make him proud, and to do that I need to follow his rules. Daddy initiates playtime. His eyes trace over me. Up and down. Up and down. I wait.

"I'm not sure you understand the concept yet, Daisy." He lifts a hand and rubs his chin as he glares down at me.

"I do. I promise, I do."

"No. I think you need a lesson."

Oh. Actually, he's right. I don't understand this concept at all. I definitely need a lesson. But do we have time? And what about the girls? What if they hear? What are we going to tell them? When are we going to tell them? Ever? The stress of acting nearly killed—

"I can see you're overthinking things. Let me make this easy for you, baby. Don't think. Just do as I say."

I nod rapidly because that's what I want more than anything right now. I don't want to think anymore or agonize about everything. It's exhausting and draining and I've been doing it for so many years—it leaves a taste in the back of my mouth like acid reflux, a sour burn.

"Kneel down."

I use the guest chair in his office to help me lower myself to my knees on his rug.

"Crawl to me."

Embarrassed, I glance up at him, but the intensity in his molten brown eyes and the way his cock is tenting his slacks as he strokes it radiates just how turned on he gets when I listen to him and do as he says. He likes to test me just as much as I like the mindless, hazy lust I feel when he tells me what to do … and the surge of power I feel when I see how it drives him wild.

I lick my lips and note the way his eyes follow the movement, his fingers curling over himself and gripping harder as I start to crawl around the right side of his desk. Each slide of my knees makes my jean skirt pull tight, the globes of my ass slowly becoming visible, the thong I'm wearing rasping against my skin as my thighs slide forward.

"God, that ass," he whispers, but the sound carries, and I grin when I hear it.

"It's your ass," I tell him.

"Damn right it is," he retorts immediately.

When I reach his feet, I sit back on my heels, staring at the rug, waiting for further instruction. I'm half-certain he's going to pull out his cock and have me suck him off again, then send me off to my date with his cum still sliding down my throat.

I rub my thighs together. A girl can only hope.

But Daddy doesn't unzip. He gently cups my chin with a calculating look as he says, "I know that was hard. You did really well crawling to me, sweetheart. So hot."

Pleasure swirls up through my belly because I love having his approval, especially after all that anxiety over what he might say about tonight.

"I wanted to give you something before you go." His touch falls away and he turns to open a drawer. He pulls out a small black box and hands it to me.

It's a ring box.

I freeze and my mind goes blank because I'm not sure what to think.

"It's nothing big so don't panic." He holds up a hand as if he can physically stop any anxiety looming in my chest. I'm nervous and surprised, though his words are definitely quelling the first.

He continues, "This isn't an engagement ring. Just a trinket. But I had this ring made for you a while ago. And I want you to wear something from me tonight so you remember who you belong to."

God. The inside of my chest has popped and is fizzing over like a bottle of champagne. Confetti flutters around inside my head … my entire body is doing some strange celebration because Gunnar Strong is marking me.

As if I could forget I'm his.

I swallow a squeal as I carefully open the box. Inside is a plain silver ring. I pull it from the velvet-covered foam and realize there's an inscription inside. A tiny, minuscule stamped teddy bear sits next to the words. *Not supposed to be easy. But worth it.*

Holy fuck.

When I glance up at him through my thick false lashes, I see him gritting his teeth almost as if he regrets giving this to me, regrets being this vulnerable.

I slide the ring onto my right ring finger. Of course, it fits perfectly. And I love how it looks so innocent and simple on the outside, but inside it's a whole different story. Just like us.

I reach up and squeeze his hand. "Thank you. God, thank you, Gunnar. I love it." I don't use his pet name. I use his real name, because I'm not playing and I want him to know that I mean every word.

He gives a stiff nod. "You'd better get going."

"Do I have to?" I breathe, jutting out my lower lip. If he hasn't said he's going, then this whole night is a waste of time.

"Yes." His expression immediately turns cold and domineering. "You do."

"But I don't want to."

"Daddy wants you to," he counters, stepping closer and grabbing my hand, placing it over the bulge in his pants. "I want to watch you through the bookshelves and give you orders until I'm ready to fuck you senseless."

Shit. Damn. Yes. I press my thighs together and feel the evidence of my own arousal. I might have just ruined these panties.

What Daddy wants, he's going to get.

DAISY

"*A*nd X is?" Justin asks, leaning unnecessarily over my paper, his gaze dropping to my breasts. Daddy texted me to cross my arms underneath them and prop them up so this *little shit*—his words—gets an eyeful.

I'm doing as ordered. It's working for Justin, which makes me nervous, even though it also gives me a dirty little thrill to see his brown eyes keep slipping down over my skin. I only hope it's working for Gunnar too. My nipples are hard little points inside my bra as I pretend to focus on math instead of the needy ache between my thighs that's been getting worse for the past hour.

Justin and I are up on the third floor of the library at a long wooden table with reading lamps with green glass shades and wooden chairs that are so uncomfortable that I don't know how anyone gets any studying done here. Based on the fact that Justin and I are the only two people on this floor, I doubt most other college students study here at all. Coffee shops are way more comfortable.

If it weren't for the game that Daddy and I are playing, my ass and brain would both be numb from this experience. But I like being his little doll and posing for him. It turns me on to think that he's out there in the stacks snapping photos of me or touching himself.

Guilt does gnaw me a bit for what we're doing with Justin, because he's a decent guy, but the mind's power to rationalize anything and everything makes me realize that tonight I'm getting far more of a lesson in psychology than math. I'm twisted. Far more unkind and unhinged than I ever thought I was. But then, any girl who stands in a corner half-naked to seduce her stepfather isn't entirely sane.

I'm okay with that.

More than okay.

Another text comes through.

Spread your legs, baby girl.

My breath hitches as I do as instructed, widening my stance as far as my tight jean skirt will allow. *Fuck, Daddy's dirty.* Quivering pulses work their way from my core to my thighs as I look up from the table, eyes studying the stacks, wondering if he's straight across from us in the dusty old books.

Sure enough, on the second shelf up from the floor, I see a shadow appear as first one book then another slides from its resting spot. My heart starts pounding. He *is* looking. I squirm on my seat as I picture him kneeling on the floor, staring right between my legs.

"That problem getting to you?" Justin leans over to look at my work, his hair flopping over his forehead in a way some other girl might find cute.

"No. Um. It's not the problem. I just remembered something." I drag my phone up from my lap. "I need to shoot off a quick text, sorry. Grocery list thing."

"Sure. Sure." He gives me an easy grin.

You are making me crazy.

Immediately, a text bubble pops up on my screen and three little dots appear as Gunnar types. And types. And types. *What the hell?* My breath starts coming more quickly as I stare at the phone wondering what he could possibly want to say.

When the message comes through, I want to scream, because I think he was toying with me. Typing and erasing. Typing and erasing. Making me wait.

All that he ends up sending is this: *Pull your panties to the side.*

Ugh. Jerk. I glare off into the stacks, hoping that my gaze cuts right into his chest. *Mean Daddy. Mean.*

Part of me wants to be a brat and close my legs entirely, but I like this game far more than I like my pride.

"All good on the grocery front?" Justin asks.

"Oh. Um. Yup." I give him a strained, toothy grin as I put my phone back on my lap, balancing it on my thigh while my fingers yank the hem of my skirt up underneath the table. "Did you try out sixty-six though? That one is kind of a mind bender."

Justin leans back over his textbook to find the problem I mentioned and I use his distraction to grab the gusset of my panties, which is soaked. I deftly slide it over until it hits my right thigh. The cool air-conditioning hits me with startling force from a nearby vent. I want to suck air in through my teeth at the sensation but I don't. I hold still for Daddy.

Another book disappears from that low shelf, the black shadow getting bigger. My eyes might be playing tricks on me, but I think I see movement.

How much longer? I beg silently with my eyes for him to end this game. I love it, but I'm also impatient for what comes next.

Gunnar staggered our exits from the house so the girls wouldn't get suspicious, and so he's only been texting me orders for about forty minutes which, based on his movie night shenanigans, is nothing for him, but dammit, I'm ready to be done.

I need his fingers on me. I need his mouth hovering over my pussy the way he did the other night, breathing on me and warming up every nerve ending until he dove right down and made me deranged with pleasure.

"Oh, yeah. Sixty-six is pretty complicated. Here. I'll write it out for you."

"Thanks." I'm not even sure my fake grin is holding up anymore because I think I'm nearing my breaking point. If Daddy doesn't call this off soon, I'm going to have to make some excuse to run away from this guy or risk humping my chair in public.

Justin's just not for me. I'm sure some girl might like him. But he's bored me to death tonight with tales of the video game tournament he and the other guys in his dorm just had. I faked admiration when he told me he got second place.

I bet he didn't do a victory dance nearly as adorable or embarrassing as Gunnar did the other day. A small smile crosses my lips when I think of how I get to see a different side of him than anyone else.

He doesn't act silly most of the time. Just with me. And that makes those moments all the more precious.

I drop my panties back in place, because Daddy didn't say how long I had to leave them open and it's starting to look weird that I'm not at least trying to work on the problems. I try to solve number sixty six, scratching out a few lines of the equation and then fiddling with my new ring.

Just looking at the silver gleam beneath the light makes elation bubble up in my belly. It drives me to widen my legs just a little further and even drag one of my feet up and down my chair leg suggestively. *Come on, Daddy. Hurry up.*

I glance at the stacks in front of us, wondering if he's still crouched there or if he's moved on. The books are back in place. My eyes dart all over the shelf, looking for a new opening. *Where is he now?*

Is he taking more pictures of me?

Is he jerking himself off right now? I grin naughtily, hoping he is.

"You're doing great," Justin beams down at me and I realize he thinks my smile is for him. *Shit.*

When he leans closer and I notice he's sliding his arm around the back of my seat. I'm leaning forward, so he's not quite touching me. But I'm boxed in, and I don't like it. I don't mind teasing a little or putting on a show for Daddy, but I really don't want this boy touching me.

On my thigh, my phone vibrates. I clear my throat and quickly glance down.

Come to Daddy.

Oh, thank God. I bite my lip and slide my right foot away. "I need to use the restroom. I'll be right back."

Justin's face immediately falls. "Oh, okay."

I think he was about to make a move. Perfect timing.

Relief surges out of me in a gust of air as I clutch my phone and scurry away, turning into the aisle behind the nearest stack of books in order to escape his gaze. *God, that was close. Too close.*

I lean my head back against the shelf for just a second, catching my breath as adrenaline surges through me. So when an arm touches mine, I startle and jump.

"Shhh, it's just me, baby girl," Gunnar whispers.

My entire being calms just at the sound of his voice. It's the same tone he's used to soothe me whenever I was upset over the past year, which was too damn often. I open my eyes and turn to look at him.

"Did I do a good job, Daddy?"

"Does it feel like you did a good job, baby?" he grabs my free hand and shoves it against his crotch. Through his pants, I can feel how hard he is.

I love that I do that to him.

"Follow me. Since this is a study date, I have some things to teach you …."

I stifle a moan as he pulls my hand away from his dick and turns, striding down the aisles so quickly that I have to nearly run to keep up with him. Anticipation is bubbling up happily inside of me. I can't wait to learn everything he wants to show me.

We reach a series of reading rooms that are separated from the rest of the library by a wall and oversized windows allowing outsiders to peer in. I'm guessing they were designed that way so librarians can keep an eye on the precious first editions they bring up from the archives. Or to discourage the rooms from being used for any purpose other than studying. But if they hadn't wanted people to use these rooms for hookups, they really should have stationed a permanent librarian desk right across from them, not left them alone on this floor.

Poor choice, as Gunnar would say. *Poor logic.* But I'm thrilled right now about their poor choices, because now I get to make some poor choices of my own. Some very exciting ones.

A study room at the far end is lit up bright yellow, some guy curled over a massive book, laptop glowing beside him. He has on headphones. Hopefully, we'll stay quiet enough not to disturb him. Maybe. Possibly. Honestly, right now I don't fucking care.

Gunnar heads for the study room at the opposite end of the row, four doors down. He opens the door and then pulls me inside, not bothering to turn on the light.

I can't see in the pitch black after being at the table with all the study lamps, so I end up standing still and waiting for my eyes to adjust as he walks over to the table. I hear him pull out a chair. Then there's the rasp of his zipper. A rustle of cloth. The chair groans when he sits.

"Daisy, get undressed," Daddy tells me.

"Um ..." I glance at the window of the study room. We're even more exposed here than we were in that empty classroom. What's a narrow window in a door compared with a window that spans the length of the study room and showcases everything from the waist up.

There are only two people on this floor that I know of ... Justin and that studying guy, but still.

"Get naked now, baby girl, or I'll stuff those panties in your mouth to muffle your screams while I spank you."

Gunnar's threat makes me move quickly. I kick off my heels and quickly shed my crop top and bra. Then I wriggle out of my jean skirt and panties in one go.

The cool air of the library prickles my skin as I make my way over to his chair, where his silhouette sits rigid and straight. Gunnar's still fully clothed on top. Only I'm exposed for anyone walking by to see. I'm starting to think he likes it that way.

Based on the flash of heat flaring in my low belly, I'm starting to think I might too.

"Sit on Daddy's lap."

I walk over and stand in front of him, facing the wooden table before slowly lowering myself down onto him. Gunnar guides himself so his cock slides right between my thighs and up over the front of my slit. It's so warm and hot against my skin—it's everything I've been craving from him. I end up rocking my hips automatically and his hands come down to the tops of my thighs.

I love our size difference, how his hands can cover so much of my legs as I writhe on top of him, the way his big arms surround me, how I can lean back against his chest and feel so small.

"Daisy …" he's slow and draws my name out in the most deliciously sensual way before adding, "who's supposed to start playtime?"

Immediately, I stop moving, though my pussy wants to shriek in protest because I just got his dick wet enough for the glide to feel delicious. *Dammit.* My lower lip juts out and I want to pout even though what spills out of my mouth is, "Sorry, Daddy. I've been thinking about this the entire time and I couldn't help myself."

"Good girls have self-control, baby. Now, are you my good girl? Or are you a little slut?" His hands move up to tweak my nipples and my mind blanks—I nearly forget he's spoken until he repeats it. Apparently, it wasn't a rhetorical question.

"Can I be both?" I whimper as he pinches rhythmically, making my body sing.

"You want Daddy to treat you like his own little slut? You want me to shove you under my desk at home and make you blow me while I'm working? You want me to finger you at stoplights and make you come while strangers watch?"

His naughty words alone make me want to writhe again and I whimper, reaching down and digging my fingernails into his hips as I try to resist.

"Yes."

"Are you sure?" His hands leave my nipples and one of them goes down to glide along my soaked opening while the other comes up and gathers up my hair into a low ponytail at the base of my neck. He tugs gently on my hair, turning my head to the side so he can lean down and place gentle kisses along my neck as he asks, "You wouldn't rather I wake you up each morning with sweet kisses to your little pussy?" His fingers swirl lightly around my clit. "You don't want me to make soft love to you and cuddle after?"

"Daddy!" I squeal, because between his touch and his words I'm so close to detonation. I just need a tiny bit more ….

"Which one, baby?"

"Slut. Right now, I want to be your slut." The admission flies from my lips as I give into temptation and swivel against his dick.

In under a second, he stands up and shoves me forward onto the study table. My hands fly out to catch myself and the cold wood startles my peaked nipples, contrasting the flush of heat that spreads through me knowing I'm finally about to get fucked. Hard.

Gunnar's hand doesn't leave my hair—if anything, his grip tightens.

I hear his pants drop and then, without preamble, his dick breaches me.

I gasp at the stretch—it's still new to me.

"That's it. Take, baby." He slowly slides in further and I bite my lip because the feeling is so intense.

I bite my lip and a tiny whimper escapes.

He stops pressing in, his hand reaches around to my clit and starts gently stroking up and down. "Here, Daisy, I'm going to make it all better." Slowly, he works his hand in circles and then figure eights, forgetting his own pleasure while he makes me buck.

He drops his grip on my hair. "One day, sweetie, we'll work you up to being Daddy's slut. But right now, I think you still need to be my good girl. And good girls always come first."

He pulls out and I think he grabs his dick, because he starts sliding it steadily along my seam, the hot, wet heat of it gliding over my opening while his other hand gradually builds up the intensity with my clit.

I end up pushing up from the table with my hands and arching my back as he works my body up to a frothing, needy mess. It feels so damned good that the instinct to piston my hips takes over, but Daddy steps in closer, pinning me to the table.

"Baby, stay still and just enjoy."

Fuck. I can't. He's asking the impossible. I end up reaching down and tweaking my own nipples. It adds to the build up, but Gunnar's pace is just a fraction too slow.

"Faster, please," I beg.

"No." Daddy's answer is short and curt. "My little girl doesn't get half-assed orgasms. You're going to come so hard you scream, or you're not coming at all."

He's so hot and so mean.

I drop my hands from my chest and claw at the table because his words twist me up so tight. I'm ready. I'm there. Except his fingers won't take me over the brink.

"Tell me how long you've dreamt about this, Daisy. How long have you wanted me to touch you?"

"Since the first day we met," I admit, wondering why he's distracting me from the delectable sensations fluttering through my lower belly right now.

"Did you ever touch yourself and pretend it was me?"

My cheeks shouldn't blush red hot at the admission, because he already knows the answer, but they do. "Yes."

"What did you imagine me doing to you?"

My favorite fantasy automatically comes up inside my head. "I would think about us swimming in the pool in the backyard. I'd get out of the water and lay out in the sun."

"Mmm. What bikini were you wearing?" he asks, his finger dipping into me.

"The red one. You said you liked it once." It was the skimpiest swimsuit I owned, the back little more than a g-string, but I lost it awhile ago.

"Yes, I do like that one. Maybe I'll even let you have it back now."

"You stole it?" I gasp, both from surprise and from the fact that he's curling his finger inside of me and tapping on my g-spot.

"Yes. I didn't want you wearing it out in public. But you're getting off track. Daddy wants to hear your story. What happened after you climbed out of the pool?" His other hand comes around to my clit, circling but not quite touching it.

My mind slides back to the perfectly manicured backyard and the lounge chairs on one side of the pool. "I go lay down in a lounger and you'd tell me I needed to wear sunscreen. I'd wave you off and tell you I'm going inside in ten minutes."

"Which we both know is a lie, because you love that sunshine."

I don't bother arguing with him now because those fingers of his are pure magic. My thighs are trembling. "You'd get all grumpy like you do and go grab a bottle, marching back over. Then you'd squirt it all over me." In my head, the scene plays like a movie. Gunnar's expression, angry behind a pair of sunglasses. His chest on display, those perfect pecs drawing my eyes again and again while his swim trunks drip pool water steadily onto the sizzling concrete. My arms and legs are covered in white drizzles as I glare up at him.

"Then what?" Gunnar asks, picking up the pace slightly and making my breathing grow choppy.

It's hard to focus, but he wants to hear, so I tell him. "Then you sit down and rub in the sunscreen yourself. And I'm so shocked I let you. But when you get to my bikini bottoms, you don't stop. Your hand dips underneath and you keep rubbing." *Just like you are now. God. Yes. Right there.*

"Do you try to stop Daddy?" he whispers in my ear.

"No," I confess. "I let you play with me."

"Like this?" His thumb and forefinger rub my clit between them while his other hand keeps slowly tapping my g-spot. I have to clench my teeth to keep from screaming in pleasure.

"Yessss."

I'm not as good at dirty talk as Gunnar, but inside my head, he's holding me down as he plays, telling me to be quiet, telling me he could see how soaked I was for him from across the yard, telling me how fucking hot I am.

"Then what?" Gunnar's fingers pinch and tug at my clit now as his fingers inside fuck me quicker and harder. My hips buck against the table and the wooden feet scrape against the floor. Gunnar tugs faster and I start to whimper because suddenly the sky is falling and gravity has ceased to exist. An orgasm slams into me and my hips bounce repeatedly against the table as I fall apart with a wild howl.

When the pleasure changes from a spinning, whirling vortex back to a gentle breeze, I sigh.

Gunnar, not distracted by my orgasm in the slightest, repeats his question. "What happens in your daydream after I let you come?" He varies his pace, fingers gliding over my very slick entrance, gathering cum, and sliding back up to bring my clit right back to life.

How can he do that? I wonder, dazed.

"Daisy, I'm waiting."

But, the thing is, I don't want to answer his question. I press my lips together and shake my head because I don't want to share the part of my fantasy that almost always came next. After the orgasm. After the high had faded and the fantasy was riddled with guilt because I'd just gotten off thinking about my mother's husband. I don't want that sort of emotion to ruin this, because it could. I could easily fall down the rabbit hole, wondering if I'm a bad person.

Gunnar stills, all movement ceasing, my delicious deliriousness fading away. "What happened after that? Good girls don't keep secrets."

My hands fist on top of the table and my neck curls down in shame. I don't want to tell him, but I also don't want to disobey him. "You'd tell me it was my fault you touched me. That I tempted you. It was my fault and it was going to ruin the family."

The guilt and fear that have been simmering underneath the surface of my happiness for the past several days erupt into a sob that I try to choke back. The fantasy isn't real. And neither is the guilt scenario, not anymore at least because he isn't technically married anymore. But feelings don't often have a basis in reality ... look at how long I pined for Gunnar not knowing if he wanted me back.

Immediately, Gunnar's hands move. He slides out from inside me and his big strong arms wrap around my torso before he turns me around to face him. His palms come up to cradle my face, fingers still slick from being inside me, and his lips drop to my forehead. "I would *never* blame you. Ever. If anything, I blame myself, because you're so fucking irresistible that right and wrong blur."

A tear slips out of my right eye and his face wavers in my vision. "Are we ... wrong?" I asked it this morning, we literally already had this conversation and I feel foolish bringing this topic up again but I am ... because after the memory of that guilt ... I feel vulnerable and unsure.

Gunnar presses a soft kiss to my forehead, then the tip of my nose before he says, "No, Daisy. We're not wrong. Nothing in the world has ever felt more right. We know it. She does too. She's happy for us. We're different than what people expect ... but there is absolutely nothing wrong with us. Want to know a secret?" He gently swipes at my tears to ensure that I'm looking up at him clearly. "I'm sick and twisted and perverse. I've had goddamned dirty thoughts about you forever. Much worse than by the pool, baby. But fucked up thoughts? Fantasies? Everybody has them. You know what everyone doesn't have? Someone to help make them come true. Someone brave enough to let you live them out.

Someone sweet enough to kneel down in front of you in and let you fuck their face as rough as you want."

I give a broken laugh. "*And ... you ruined it.*"

"I might not be poetic, little girl. But, you're the other half of my soul."

His lips capture mine and his kiss doesn't just reassure me, it flows through me and washes away all the uncertainties and fears that have been festering inside. Because I believe he means those words with every fiber of his being. I melt into him, twining my arms around his neck and sinking into his affection. His affirmation. The honest truth of his confession that we both need each other and fulfill one another in ways nobody else ever could.

For a few minutes, the outside world ceases to exist. Gunnar and I are the only people on the entire planet and we're melding breaths, molding one another's flesh with our fingers, trying desperately to use touches to erase the lines between his existence and mine and combine ourselves into one.

He grabs my ass and lifts me until I'm off the table, legs wrapping around him as he spins and walks forward. Suddenly, I find myself pinned to the window of the study room, the cold glass pressing against my back as Gunnar lines his dick up and shoves into me—hard.

He sets a brutal pace then, one that makes the glass thump repeatedly. His pelvis smashes into mine and his fingers dig into the bottoms of my thighs and I've never hurt more or felt more free.

Because I belong to him.

Because I trust him.

I let myself go—my mind floating off above the Earth. I glimpse the sun. I see solar flares. But then I realize those are streaks of red dancing behind my eyelids as I get fucked within an inch of my life by the most perfect man in the world.

When Gunnar orders, "Come for Daddy, baby," I do.

GUNNAR

I drive home with a huge fucking grin on my face. I never, not in my wildest dreams, thought Daisy would be this perfect. I thought I'd have to be slow with her … seduce her gradually, introduce kinks in tiny little stages. The dark craving for her made me okay with being very slow and deliberate, not just jumping right into what I wanted.

But I didn't need to do any of that.

My baby girl wanted her Daddy. And she just might be as kinky as me.

Fuck, I only came half an hour ago and just the thought of her makes me start to get hard. Well, alright, it's not just the thought of her. I'm also pretty fucking stoked that scrawny little Justin saw me banging the shit out of Daisy in the study room. The twerp's face had gone pale and angry for a second before he'd flipped me off.

When I got into medical school, I thought that was the best moment of my life. When I successfully extracted my first tumor, that moment eclipsed all others. Then I thought it was meeting Daisy. But nothing, nothing trumps roughly owning my girl in front of another man.

That wasn't even on my list of kinks before. But it sure as hell is now.

Maybe I should feel a sliver of regret. A normal person might. But fucking my Daisy in front of him, knowing he could see her delectable ass through the window and realize he was never getting a piece of it, made my dick swell twice as much as normal.

God, I don't think I've ever nutted that hard in my entire life.

We're definitely doing that again.

When I pull into the garage, I spot Daisy's car already parked in its spot. I knew she made it home safely because I tracked her on my phone, but seeing her car just eases the tension inside my chest. I have no doubt that seeing her in person will ease it further, because in addition to owning her, I have a driving desire to see her safe.

I wonder what she's doing right now. If she's curled up on her bed, legs tucked underneath her, making up lies for her friends about how the date was lame. I wonder if her little pussy is sore. It has to be after that pounding I gave her.

I shove open my car door and smile because I know exactly how I'm going to check on her. While she slept the other night, I made a few little changes to the house.

The TV screen hung on the wall in my office shows several rooms in the house and I lean forward from my seat at my desk, eyes scanning only to see all of her friends gathered in the living room. I click that room off, uninterested, because I quickly spot Daisy in the shower in her en-suite.

Much more interesting.

The glass door of the shower is unfortunately steamy, so I can't see her full figure, but her silhouette, and that ass that drives me crazy, are enough. I wonder if she's trying to wash the scent of sex off her—since I made her come home with my cum still dripping out of her.

God, everything about her just screams sex to me.

I touch myself through my pants, though I know there's no chance I'll be getting any while her friends are here. Not unless I sneak in and grab Daisy while they're sleeping.

Not going to happen since I don't want to traumatize her. But even if I can't have her again tonight, I love knowing that there's going to be a next time. And a time after that. And another one after that.

Now that I have her, I'm never letting her go, not even if I have to chain her—

"We can't get the remote—WHAT THE FUCK IS THAT?"

I glance up and see Rose, Daisy's best friend, standing in front of my desk, dumbstruck—staring at the TV. On the screen, a very naked Daisy wraps a towel around herself.

Aw shit.

The girl takes one look at my hand on my dick and storms out. *Guess it was a good thing I left my pants on.* I roll my eyes as I shut down the camera app and TV and go to follow the screaming little vixen down the hall.

What's Daisy going to think? Is she going to be hurt? Are these girls going to hate us and make her cry?

Goddammit. Of course, it had to be this way. I knew things were going too well. Chaos had to descend eventually. Daisy and I don't get to announce our decision to date in a month, holding hands and looking like a prim and proper sweet little couple. Her friend has to catch me in the middle of a kink.

I sigh, running a hand through my hair, pissed at myself once again. If my goal in life is not to traumatize Daisy then I just messed up big time. Failing seems like it's becoming a habit of mine and that is simply unacceptable.

When I reach the living room, I see Rose has already rallied the troops and the other Wild Flowers are standing with their arms folded, eyes judgmental.

"Creep," Lily mutters.

"Pervert," Rose snarls.

Violet only looks at me with raised eyebrows, as if she's impressed, which instantly makes her my new favorite. At least she's giving me the benefit of the doubt.

"I'm getting Daisy," Violet announces.

"Be gentle when you tell her, please," I say, relieved Rose didn't run right into the bathroom screaming.

Rose's eyes hurl daggers in my direction as she gives Violet her own set of directions. "Good. Tell her she can come stay at my house—"

"She's not going anywhere," I interject. Seriously, Rose is taking things too far. She's blowing this out of proportion. Her face is blotchy with fury and her hands are shaking as she raises them and pantomimes strangling me.

God. My preference for sneaking around and nearly getting caught has really come back to bite me. My own fault. This is a disaster and I'm unprepared. I researched the shit out of dom/sub relationships but announcing a taboo relationship? Didn't do that. Didn't think it would ever happen. Now, look where I am.

I glance down the hall, toward the stairs that lead up to the bedrooms. My girl doesn't appear … I assume she's getting dressed.

"You're her stepfather!" Lily mutters, breaking the silence.

"Actually, former stepfather," I reply. "And she's an adult."

"And he's hot," Violet adds from down the hall, her voice echoing off the walls. She's definitely my favorite.

The other two are unconvinced. Apparently, my hotness doesn't erase my clandestine activities.

"You fucking married her mother!" Rose shouts as if I've forgotten my past legal commitments. She's most definitely forgotten they're past.

"Yes." My reply is calm, but only because I can't let Daisy see me shouting at her friends. It's not fair to put her in the middle of a heated argument. She's probably going to be embarrassed enough to admit the truth, though that does make me wonder if any part of her regrets what we're doing, especially since she's brought up her guilt twice now. I know she's already torn about her mother, but could her friends' judgment tip the scales?

My chest tightens up.

I just got her. I can't lose her.

Not over something as stupid as a few laws. Some signatures on a piece of paper. I need to convince her friends that this isn't a big deal.

"Darla was a good woman. But it's not like we had a love match. My attraction to Daisy is—"

"I don't give a shit that you're attracted to her. You were filming her without her permission!" Lily's cheeks are as white as her namesake flower.

Technically, she's half correct. Daisy and I had a conversation about my proclivities, but I haven't told her yet about the cameras I set up while she was sleeping.

Will she mind? Will that be the dealbreaker? I squeeze my eyes shut, because it feels like someone just dove right into my chest and is performing open heart surgery on me while I'm conscious.

"You're a peeping Tom. Is that it?" Rose tosses a hand out to the side, gesturing in the direction of my office. "How long have you been watching her?"

I don't respond. My eyes are on the stairs. I don't owe explanations to these girls. I only owe them to my girl. And I need to see how this is affecting her. How I hurt her. I consider running up the stairs to her room, but she might be so angry at me she won't want to see me. And I don't want to unintentionally intimidate her into a decision.

Will she forgive me?

Will she even want to tell them about us now? Is there still an us?

"You sick fuck!" Rose shouts and tears spring to her eyes.

She's crying?

I glance over at Lily, bewildered about the intensity of Rose's reaction. It seems over the top, but Lily looks just as taken aback as I do. Her hand tentatively goes to Rose's shoulder, but Rose shrugs it off, pointing a threatening finger at me "Don't you dare even talk to Daisy—"

Daisy emerges from the hall wearing only a plush white robe that ends at her calves. Violet is trailing behind her, a shocked and dazed look on her face.

My girl's face is much calmer than I realize, her blue eyes seeking me out. As soon as our gazes connect, the fierce burn in my chest recedes and I can breathe again. Seeing her, I just know we're going to be okay.

Something soft and bright takes up residence inside my ribs.

Then my girl breaks eye contact and scurries across the front entryway over to Rose. "Rosie! I love you for defending me. But stop. You don't know what you're talking about!"

"Yes, she does! Nobody with good intentions fucking videotapes people in their own home. He's a creep!" Rose declares.

She's not wrong. I did have dirty intentions for Daisy from the moment I met her. I didn't just want to fuck her. I wanted to be her Daddy. I wanted to dominate her. Own her. I still do. Daisy brings out something in me nobody else ever has.

But in addition to domination, Daisy brings out a tenderness in me I've never had before. She makes this demon inside me worse. But she also makes other parts of me better.

I'm not going to let Rose's disapproval dissuade me for a second though, because in an unbelievable twist of fate—one that Rose certainly won't want to hear, Daisy actually wants twisted things from me as much as I want to give them to her.

The monster inside my chest purrs at that fact.

My eyes drift over to Lily, whose gaze is flitting back and forth between my girl and me as if she's trying to decide if I'm somehow secretly pulling Daisy's strings. God, I've known I've been fucked in the head for years, but watching these other girls villainize me with their looks makes me want to fucking declare that I love Daisy to them before I've even told her. I won't, because she deserves better.

But I want to because it would smack that judgment right off their faces. If they'd been inside my head … no that would probably make matters worse. But if they'd been inside my heart ….

I want to curl my hand into a fist, but I don't want them to perceive me as threatening so I force my muscles to relax, force myself to think of the way Daisy looked when she sat on my lap and first surrendered to me—so sweet and vulnerable.

Nothing's worth risking the way she looks at me. The awe that crosses her features, which is only mirrored by my own. I'm not going to let anger or indignation threaten that.

I stare calmly back at Lily until she glances away. I have no clue what she's thinking, if I've already been convicted in her head the way I have in Rose's. I decide to focus my energy back on my girl, watching for some sign of what she needs as she deals with the nuclear fallout here.

Daisy finally gets Rose to quiet down before turning and looking at me. Her huge blue eyes are soulful and pleading, and I know immediately that she's asking for permission to tell them. Didn't she already tell Violet?

My gaze swings to the blonde-haired girl, who's still standing at the far side of the room and looking smug.

Daisy's face must have given it all away; her expressions do that sometimes—project exactly what she's thinking. Violet figured it out.

It's time the rest do too. Maybe it will lessen their vitriol. Not quite excuse what I've done, but make it a little less ... disturbing. I give a single nod.

"Gunnar and I ... we're seeing each other."

It's one of those mic drop moments. Or perhaps it's a little more sinister. It's the drop of a pin just pulled from a grenade.

Rose explodes, her manicured nails flying to her curly hair. "WHAT THE FUCK?"

Lily's eyebrows scrunch. "What about your date tonight?"

Daisy blushes fire-engine red as Violet gapes, eyes darting between us before she asks me, "You didn't get called in for a surgery, did you?"

I don't have to respond. She puts two and two together easily enough, her shaking head turning to my girl in admiration. "Damn. I might be jealous right now, Daise, he's a fox."

I need to ask Daisy when her birthday is. Violet is getting some champagne.

"No. No! You cannot ... he's *crossed* a line!" Rose bursts out, arm slashing through the air to emphasize her point.

I turn to Daisy, staring deeply into her eyes. "Did I ever disrespect you or make you feel unsafe?" *Outside of hot sex where I push your boundaries?* "Haven't I always put your needs first?" *Even when I wanted so badly to date you but I knew you were too emotionally ripped apart to handle it?*

"You've always been amazing," Daisy responds in a whisper, a blush painting her beautiful cheeks.

That right there, that soft, tender look … it's worth everything.

"I'm sorry it came out this way. But, Daisy … I would rip my own heart out before I'd try and hurt you."

"I know you would. Because you've proven it a million times." Her eyes become damp as her soft voice fills the otherwise silent entryway. "You came into my life when I needed you most. When I had nothing, you gave me everything. You have been there for me through thick and thin. God, Gunnar … you've been there through the worst." She laughs shakily, bringing her fist to her mouth like she's trying to stifle a sob. When she has control of her voice again, she speaks, though the sound is tightly strung like a violin. "You've made me laugh, held me when I cried. Out of all the people in the entire world, I'm so glad I met you. I've never looked at vending machines the same." She gives a teary chuckle, which I hear echoed in my own throat.

God, I fucking love her.

Inside my chest—there are church bells, bubbles and sparklers, hundreds of doves released into the sky.

Because to me … it sounds like she just spoke her vows.

I step forward and take her hand, lifting it up to my lips. I kiss the ring I gave her as I stare into her shining eyes. "I'd do anything for you. You're my world."

"Aww," Lily's attitude softens, tossing a hand over her heart, but I don't even glance at her. I don't have eyes for anyone but my girl.

Mine.

"It's a fucking trick! Don't believe it!" Rose is still screaming. The girl is literally unhinged.

I glance over at Daisy, who turns to gaze at Rose in concern. "Rosie, honey. It's not a trick. I started all of it. I came on to him. Gunnar would never …."

She's wrong. I would. But whatever she needs to say to calm her friend down.

Rose doesn't listen. She just shakes her head as tears spill from her eyes. Then, without warning, she bolts down the hall, yanking open the front door and disappearing into the night. We all stare at the gaping door and the black shadows creeping into the house for a moment—shock rippling through the room.

What just happened?

"I'd better follow her." Lily bites her lip and gives us all an apologetic smile before trotting off after Rose.

"Fuck!" Daisy brings a fist to her forehead, tears coming to her eyes.

"You can say that again. About all of this," Violet gestures at the room in general.

"I'm sorry, Daisy." I can't help but touch her cheek, caress her shoulder, reassure her anyway I can.

She leans into my palm and blinks up at me. "It will all be alright?" She makes the phrase into a question.

I cup her face gently. "Yes. It will all be alright. I have you and you have me and so everything will be alright."

She nods against my hand, her skin so soft and delicate. I want to kiss her, so I do, but just gently, just a light brush of our lips to reassure us both.

When I lean back, I bring our moment to a close because my control freak nature cannot stand the thought of those girls wandering outside without coats. Rose is clearly having some kind of breakdown but they're going to end up with hypothermia if we don't do something soon. "It's January. Neither of those girls wore a coat or took a flashlight." I point at Violet. "You, follow me and I'll get stuff for all of you." Then I point at Daisy. "Go get dressed."

"Yes, Daddy," slips out before she can help it. She gives a little dismayed squeak before she runs off down the hall.

Violet smirks at me as she follows me to the coat closet. "So it's like that, huh? Knew you were a kinky fucker. Just knew it."

I turn and glare at her. "Violet—if you bug or embarrass Daisy about this, your new spot as my favorite will be revoked. And the birthday trip Daisy was going to plan for you—" I'm improvising at this point, but I snap my fingers as though the trip is going to disappear.

Violet shuts right up.

I sigh and turn back to the closet door, which squeaks annoyingly as I pull it open. "God-fucking-dammit."

"Not how you wanted this night to end, huh?"

"Not exactly." I grab three thick coats, shoving them into her arms before reaching up onto the shelf to swipe some flash-lights. As I check the first one, clicking it on to ensure it works, she shrugs on a jacket.

"You do know that if you break her heart, we'll have to kill you." Violet delivers the line with absolutely no-nonsense, as if she believes she's actually capable of murder.

I resist the urge to snort sarcastically in response, because her sentiment is serious, even if her threat isn't. I gesture with a flashlight toward the hallway that holds the steps up to my girl's room. "She's far more likely to break me than I am her. I fell a long time ago and she's barely started rolling down the hill."

And it's true.

Daisy might have had a crush before. She might even love me now—based on that public profession that I'm going to replay daily in my head for the rest of my life, I'm pretty sure she does. That knowledge fills up a hole inside of me I didn't even know existed. But I've long passed the point of love and crossed into the territory of obsession. One day, she might join me. But with Daisy … I'll happily take whatever I can get, just like I always have.

Violet, thinking my declaration is far more innocent, just smiles. "Good to hear."

She gathers the flashlights from my hands and then strides toward the front door. I follow her and close it gently behind her as she heads off down the xeriscaped front yard to find her friends.

"Daddy?" Daisy's voice echoes through the front hall.

I turn to see her wet hair piled into a messy bun on top of her head. She's wearing yoga pants and a wolf sweatshirt and biting her lip nervously.

I open my arms and she runs into them so hard it sets me back half a step. Her hug around my waist is brutal, but I

185

revel in it—because she's coming to me for comfort, just the way she should.

I reach down and nock my index finger underneath her chin, tilting her beautiful face up toward me. Her freckles are more pronounced without makeup and I make a plan to kiss each and every one. Tomorrow. After this has all simmered down.

"You need a hat before you go outside with that wet hair."

Her lips wobble. "I don't know what's going on with Rose. I'm sorry—"

"I'm sorry I wasn't more discreet," I offer. I don't apologize for staring at her in the shower, because I'm not sorry about that at all.

Daisy shakes her head. "I would have had to tell them eventually, right?"

"Yup. I wouldn't let you keep me your dirty little secret forever."

She gives a half-assed giggle, rolling her eyes, and I give her another tight squeeze before turning and walking back over to the coat closet.

"Why do you think she freaked out?"

I shrug, though I have my suspicions. People lash out harder after they've been hurt themselves. I think little Ms. Rose might be hiding something. But if she hasn't told Daisy … well, people keep secrets for a reason.

I did.

"I think she needs you to ask her," I say as I grab a knitted turquoise beanie for my girl to wear. I also pull out a scarf and her heavy coat, because I'm not about to let her get sick.

"Are you … are you mad?" she asks, voice tight.

I spin around quickly to look at her. "Baby, I could never be mad at you, though I do blame you completely for being so irresistible."

That earns me a little smile that only widens when I carefully slide the winter hat over my girl's head and carefully arrange it to ensure it covers her ears, which I know are sensitive to cold.

"I'm sorry about this," she repeats and gestures vaguely at the front door as if it's her fault.

"Don't be silly," I tell her, helping her shrug her puffy pink jacket over her shoulders.

"I knew people would be shocked. But I didn't think us being together was going to be—"

"So dramatic? That's on me." I interject as I lasso her with the scarf and pull her close. I lean down, unable to resist her lips. Just a quick brush. Then another. The monster inside me wants to shove her against the wall and keep her here, telling the world to go fuck themselves. But I pull back before I get carried away. "Tonight sucks, honey. I'm sorry about it. But all I can say is I hope, in the long run, it's worth it." I reach out and touch the ring I put on her finger, a precursor to the other one I fully plan to give her when she's ready.

Her resulting smile gleams like a jewel. "True. I'm glad you think so because it might take her a while to come around to the idea."

I shrug and grab the last flashlight from the closet, handing it over to her. "Whatever it takes."

Daisy beams up at me and I grin right back. *Rose will get used to the idea. She'll have to,* I reason, as I watch my girl saunter around me toward the front door. Because this thing between Daisy and I ... it's as forever as forever fucking gets.

1 WEEK LATER

DAISY

*G*iddy energy ripples through me as I eye Gunnar's navy lunch bag on the passenger seat of my car. He forgot it—which never happens. And that little bit of luck has given me the opportunity to do something I've daydreamed about for nearly two years but never, ever would have done before.

Sex in his office.

Oh, god. Even just thinking about what's about to happen has my thighs tensing in anticipation.

Will he like me just showing up? Will he be mad? Will he punish me? Will he push my limits?

I hope so. I'm kind of counting on it. Well, all except the mad bit.

My teeth dig tiny crescents into my lower lip. I check my makeup in the rearview mirror as I wait for the light in front of me to change colors. Mascara coats my lashes and I'm wearing a little bit of brown liner. Pink blush with a tiny bit of matching lip gloss complete the look. I smooth back my hair, which I curled into waves as soon as my schedule opened up and I realized that I could play delivery girl. My face looks good. Professional but innocent enough, just like the outfit I have on. A white blouse, pearl necklace, and navy skirt. But that's it.

No bra.

No panties.

I am wearing some nude pasties Rose said Lily swears by—though I'm sweating so much from nerves that I'm seriously afraid these things are going to slide right off.

No. Positive thinking only.

You've got this.

The light turns green and I get an arrow to turn into the hospital parking lot just as I start to question myself. Maybe I shouldn't be doing this. Maybe I should just have him come to the car—no. No chickening out.

He says he's not hiding what we mean to each other. So if that means the grumpy, judgy medical assistant working the front desk in his department side-eyes me, so be it. Screw Melissa.

Yeah, okay, I feel better having thought that. Screw Melissa.

I lick my lips as I pull carefully into a parking space. Then I reach over and grab his lunch and my purse, and with a squeal, I leap out of the car, scurrying over to the office entrance. The surgical clinic is technically part of the hospital, but—as with most hospitals—this place is a cobbled-together beast that's grown over the decades. The one thing I'm thankful for is the fact that my mom was never in a position to go to Gunnar's office, she was far too ill. There are no memories tainting where he works.

A glass door slides open as I near the building and I walk into a lobby filled with people wearing weary expressions. Avoiding eye contact and clutching the coat I have on a tiny bit closer, I find myself facing Melissa in less than two seconds.

A tall woman with dried out hair dyed the color of hay, Melissa has always given off a really super welcoming vibe. As in, not at all.

I give her a small smile and say, "Gunnar forgot his lunch. Can you let him know—"

"Just drop it here." Melissa doesn't even glance my way as she gestures toward a crowded corner of her desk.

"No, thank you. I'd like to see him."

Melissa does look up from the folder in her hands then. Her brown eyes feel judgy.

Trying not to have any nervous ticks, I clutch the lunch in my hands a little tighter. "Can you please call him and let him know?"

Lily would be so proud of me right now because I've always hated Melissa but I've always avoided disagreeing with her over anything. She's one of those women with a prune personality. Shrively and gross and all you want is to get away from her.

I see her swallow hard, her eyes narrowing in censure because I told her no. Surprisingly, that look from her makes my back stiffen and I stand up straighter.

"Excuse me?" She leans forward like a school teacher about to deliver a scolding.

Forgetting about my lack of panties, I take a big step forward. "Please call him for me." My tone is anything but nice because...really? Who needs to get on a power trip over a sack lunch? And why the hell wouldn't she want me talking to Gunnar.

Her nostrils flare and for a second it feels like I can see right through her skull into her thoughts. Judgment and indignation are snapping like alligators in there.

My lips open to repeat myself, but Gunnar's office door opens just then and he appears. He's wearing a white button up shirt with the sleeves rolled up and gray slacks today while he does office work. His dress shoes gleam in the overhead fluorescent lights. So do the gray streaks in his hair, which is smoothed back from his forehead. He shaved this morning, but there's already a hint of stubble at the base of his jaw as I stare at every gorgeous, delicious inch of him as he focuses on me.

The smile on my face is automatic, every muscle softening, even my heart. Even though we've kept our new status private for a little bit as we adjust (with the exception of the Wild Flower debacle last week), it amazes me that I feel the exact same mushy adoration in public. The presence of the perfect-bubble popping bitch, Melissa, doesn't seem to affect us at all, which somehow bolsters me. I didn't need reassurance about how right this thing with Gunnar is, not really, but it's nice to have it anyway. It's good to realize that no matter what's going on around us, this thing between us isn't dimming or diminishing.

In fact, it might just be growing stronger.

Is that even possible?

"I brought your lunch. You forgot it," I state in a tone that even I can recognize is sickly sweet. One that might make me cringe if I heard it from someone else. But I can't help it. Butterflies are bounding around inside of me.

"Thank you." His eyes look as hungry as the rest of him must be as he stares at me. "Want to come in?"

I nod and smile, biting my lower lip even as I grin because I can't wait to see his reaction. I'm not sure I can pull off the whole hop-on-the-desk, spread-my-legs, and declare "here's your lunch" that my fantasy hussy-self can. But I'm damn excited to play.

"Hold my calls," Gunnar tells Melissa. "Actually, go take lunch. I'll eat with my girl here and we'll keep our eyes on the phones." He reaches into his pocket and pulls out a twenty, placing it on her desk.

Tingles run up the insides of my thighs, because if he's sending off his secretary, that's a very good sign for me.

Begone, Melissa.

"Have fun!" he tells her, in a tone similar to the bossy one he uses on me. Similar, but not quite his daddy voice. I bite my lip as I realize that he reserves a special tone just for me. Maybe I should stop being surprised at how the things between us are unique. Special. Sparkles glimmer inside my chest as he comes right up to me, brushing against my side.

I don't bother to look back, but I think I can feel Melissa's eyes on me when Gunnar's hand slides along my lower back as he escorts me into his office.

Should I have said he was my boyfriend? That we're dating now? Does he want me announcing that kind of thing at work? Is he ready for that? My friends are one thing, but the whole world?

Nervous energy deflates some of my happy and horny anticipation.

Nope, don't overthink it.

The second he's closed the door behind us, I spin around and throw myself at him, peppering his neck with kisses. The smell of his aftershave is an immediate aphrodisiac.

"I missed you, Daddy."

The hand that was at my lower back digs into the top of my ass through my coat and skirt as he pulls me against him. Meanwhile, I feel him lean slightly backward and the lock on his door snicks into place. "I always miss you when you're gone," he murmurs. "But I absolutely love coming home to you."

I glow as bright as a star in the sky.

God, he's just perfect.

"Same," I sigh against his neck, lost in his sweetness for a moment and forgetting the reason I came. He's always had this way of distracting me, Gunnar. Of making me feel like nothing else exists.

"Don't you have class?"

"Canceled. Professor's sick. And the girls are busy. And you forgot your lunch so I brought you that...and a surprise."

His eyebrows shoot up and he extends his hand, holding it out for the lunch box. I hand it over, trying not to giggle with mirth as he walks over to his desk. I quickly shed my coat and hang it next to his on the hooks near his door. When I spin around I spot him unzipping the box as if he suspects the surprise is in there.

"It better not be cake," he murmurs as he flips open the lid.

"Not that kind of cake," I respond.

That gets his attention. He straightens and turns back to look at me, one eyebrow raised in question.

My throat dries out and tiny tingles shoot up my arms as I slowly reach for my skirt and lift it. Higher. Higher.

His eyes drag over me with an intensity that makes my lower belly heat. When his breath catches, mine does to. And when I bare myself to him, he curls his fingers into his hip and I swear, I can feel a phantom touch inside me, giving me a wispy ghost of the sensation I get when those fingers make the exact same motion.

"Are you being naughty, Daisy?" he whispers, voice catching slightly.

"No, Daddy. Sneaky." I use that word that tends to send him spiraling.

It has the intended effect.

Immediately, his lunch is forgotten as he stalks back over with feral intent. I love how my neck has to crane upward as he nears, the way his scent already makes the back of my knees start to weaken. His broad shoulders block out the rest of the room as he closes the gap until his body presses against mine. The fabric of his pants brushes against my inner thighs, feel the quick beat of his heart against my cheek. He raises one hand and slowly drags the tips of his fingers along my outer thigh and his light touch has me trembling. Tightening.

His brown eyes draw me in, trap me. Staring at him feels like getting caught in quicksand---except I want to be dragged under.

He leans down and his breath is warm on my ear when he says, "Sneaky girls hide under their daddy's desk."

Fuck. Immediately, I become soaked. So so ready for him. But I know how he likes to play, slow and drawn out. And that's exactly what I came for.

Nipples tightening, I want to rub up against him, but Gunnar told me what he wanted, and there's nothing hotter than letting him take a naughty fantasy to the next level for the two of us. I showed up and instigated, but now, I'm completely ready to relinquish control and let him make me float off into a deliciously blissful headspace.

Swallowing hard, I take a tiny step back and drop my skirt before I move around him to head to his desk.

"Baby girl." His voice makes me hesitate as he comes up behind me and grabs my skirt, tucking the hem up into the waistband, leaving my ass bare. "I wanna see you crawl. I want to watch you get on all fours and imagine exactly how you're going to look when I fuck you doggie later."

Molten lava takes over my stomach and I gasp at his words.

But he's not done with me. His hand sneaks forward around my stomach and he pulls me back against him. My naked ass rubs against him and I can feel the stiff outline of his cock beneath his pants as his fingers make quick work of the buttons on my blouse. Each inch of exposed skin tingles.

He rids me of my shirt and then slowly peels the stickers off each of my breasts. The tugging sensation combined with the cool air-conditioning and Gunnar's touch leave my nipples hard and sensitive---desperate to be sucked.

But not yet.

Patience.

It's the most delicious and frustrating thing Gunnar's ever taught me. He's the boss. I submit fully, totally. And when he's ready, he'll give me the most mind-blowing orgasm I've ever experienced. The most mind-blowing love.

Gunnar backs away, leaving my rucked up navy skirt and high heels on. My pearl necklace dangles as I slowly lower myself to my hands and knees, grateful that Gunnar's office has carpet, even if it's a little rough.

Then I crawl forward, breasts swaying, spurred on by the hiss of breath I hear my daddy drawing in through his teeth. I try to imagine what I look like. I know he loves my ass. I wonder if he loves teasing little glances at my pussy too as I move away from him, sliding one knee at a time. Light-headed anticipation ripples through me.

Daddy doesn't follow me around the desk, so I end up pushing his chair aside and crawling under myself, wedging my body into the cramped space, sitting back on my heels because I'm anticipating what comes next. I can't wait for him to come around, sit down, and then unzip those pants---

What I don't expect is the phone call. A ringing sound fills the office and my entire body tenses before I realize that

Gunnar just called someone on his cell phone and put it on speaker.

My breath freezes in my lungs.

Oh god. We're really sneaking. Literally. Actually.

Fuck.

"Hello?" A man's voice picks up.

"Hey, Bill. I was looking over the Styka file and wanted to see if you have a second to discuss it." I can hear the smile in Gunnar's tone; his smooth, cocky cadence is a dead giveaway about how much he's enjoying this.

"Now?"

"Yeah, I'm free if you are. About to eat lunch, but if you don't mind a quick chat…"

"Sure." The line goes dead before Gunnar hits end.

My hands fly up to cover my breasts even though there's no one in here but Gunnar to see them. Yet. My eyes dart around to the tiny strips of light visible under his desk, because the wood paneling doesn't go all the way to the carpet. Could someone else see? Could this Bill guy?

Hard and shallow, my lungs aren't certain whether we're panicking or edging right now, and they work frantically without giving me a damn bit of oxygen.

Gunnar and I have played in public at the library before. But I wasn't practically naked. Not to this degree. This…what was I thinking coming to his work? How will I live it down if one of his coworkers sees me? How will he?

My throat dries out and I barely process the opening and shutting of Gunnar's desk drawers as he puts something inside. My clothes? I hardly hear how he unlocks and opens the door to his office because cotton is filling my ears, stuffing my head full of cloudy puffs of worry.

This feels different from the library or the classroom because it's on his territory, not mine. Because if I get kicked out of school...meh. But this is his professional reputation.

Am I ruining the fantasy by pushing him into this and making it real?

If we get caught...bad things—

Trust him, Daisy. He wants you to trust him. Do you?

I take a slow, deep breath. I close my eyes. My safeword pops into my head. But the idea of using it makes my chest tighten uncomfortably.

If Gunnar trusts me to obey him and to stay under here while he has this meeting, then I want to prove I deserve that trust.

I lower my hands to my thighs and try to relax them. My stomach doesn't immediately unclench but I try to keep a slow and steady pace as I hear Gunnar's shoes pad across the carpet back to me. His legs appear in my line of sight and he sits in his chair, sliding in closer until his knees brush against my chest.

Automatically, I reach for him and ground myself by holding onto his leg.

One of his hands sneaks underneath his desk and he holds his palm out until I lean my cheek onto it, nuzzling into him.

"You're so perfect, baby," he whispers.

I drift away. I'm still here, still feel the hard press of industrial carpet against my shins. Still feel the cold air wisping across my bare ass. Still feel Gunnar's pant legs as he shifts around in his seat. But Gunnar keeps that hand on my cheek and I find myself able to shed my worry, to abandon my self-consciousness and let myself get swept up in the fantasies about all the things Gunnar might do.

Will he have me touch him while he talks to his friend? I imagine running my palm over his pants, feeling his cock stiffen and his throat clear as he tries to hide how turned on he is.

Would Gunnar let me suck him? Would he unzip his pants and let me take his cock in my mouth and hold it there as he hosts his meeting? I imagine slowly sucking him, letting my tongue slide up and down across the underside of his dick, trying to be careful not to let a single drop of precum ruin his work pants. Would I be good enough to edge him through the entire meeting? Could I be good enough to drive him to the brink so that he'd grab my face and fuck it hard the second the door closed behind Bill?

My breasts grow heavy and my nipples tighten as I imagine various scenarios, all of them ending with me watching from a bird's eye point of view as Gunnar splayed me across the top of his desk, spread my legs wide, and plunged wildly in and out of my body.

I shift one of my hands and drag the pad of my thumb over my nipple, teasing myself.

The bud grows stiff and sends a shuddering pulse of need down my belly, until my entire torso is pulsing and taut. Ready.

"Gunnar. Thanks for taking a look at that chart. Really did need a second set of eyes." Bill's tone is casual as he enters the room. His footsteps are heavy thuds that I can feel.

I try to tune him out. Focus again on how Gunnar's going to use his hands to pull my pussy lips apart and then that magical mouth of his will descend. The scruff just starting to form on his cheeks will rub roughly against my thighs as he strokes up and down each side, teasing me, refusing to touch my clit.

My pussy throbs, pulsing and needy already and the finger teasing my nipple presses down harder. I'm not certain how long I can hold out like this. Hiding under Gunnar's desk. Being his good little slut.

Fuck, maybe I can get him to call me that. Normally, that phrase would disgust me, but right now, with how wound up I am, it seems perfect.

I grow wet imagining him bending me face down over the desk, breasts pressed tight against the wood as he checks to see how wet I am, whether or not I'm a good little slut for him.

Fuck. I shift on my heels and notice exactly how wet I am. And something else. The press of my heel feels fucking good. Too far back to hit anything major and cause me to orgasm completely, if I slide my ass around on my heels, the motion still pulls and tugs at my slit in ways that are a delicious tease. My cheek inadvertently leans harder into Gunnar's hand and I think he must suspect what I'm doing because his palm stiffens.

Fuck.

I freeze as chit chat goes on above my head, muffled by the desk, trying to make out how Gunnar's tone sounds. Is he mad? I can't tell.

His hand drifts back from my cheek and then cinches around the back of my neck. I don't breathe, wondering for a second if I'm being censured. But his hand presses my head forward until I have to put my hands on his knees for balance, until my face is just in front of his crotch, my breath warm against his pants. He's most definitely hard.

He holds me in place for a second, ensuring I stay in position, before letting his hand slide down and caress my back, pushing aside my hair so that his fingers can swirl patterns across my bare skin.

Innocent touch but oh-so-naughty. Just as my lips are poised nearby but not yet around his cock.

I dig my nails into his legs slightly, just enough to let him know how wound up I am. In response, his hand glides down over my arm and gently clasps one of my breasts. The desire to surge into him is nearly overwhelming and I wonder if he knows how much control I'm exerting right now to be good for him. To please him.

I deserve the orgasm of the century for this.

His thumb and forefinger find my nipple, pinching and tugging. Making me feel quite certain I'm going to get it.

But when?

Fucking hell—when?

"Thanks." That word from Bill is louder than the rest. And suddenly, Gunnar's hand abandons my nipple and he slowly rolls himself back, giving me enough time to retreat before he stands.

"No problem. Happy to help. Now, will you shut that door? I want to grab five minutes before I've got to head to Grimsby's meeting."

"Yup." The heavy footsteps retreat, but I hardly hear them over the rapid thumping of my own heart. It's almost time. My nerve endings crackle with anticipatory excitement. Breaths come fast and shallow and I lick my lips as I wait for Daddy to summon me.

The door thumps closed and I startle in my own skin, nearly bonking my head on the underside of the desk.

But Gunnar doesn't call for me. He doesn't gesture. He stands and walks to the door and the lock clicks into place. The sound seems to echo inside my brain.

He slowly and deliberately walks back over, sits down, and undoes his belt buckle. Each tiny motion as he pulls the belt apart makes me lean forward on my hands, panting with desire. When he reaches for his zipper, I nearly lose it.

"We're going to pretend Bill's still in here," Gunnar says as he fishes himself out. He's already swollen and hard as a rock, and his thumb swipes over the head of his dick as he rolls forward, closer to me.

"Suck my cock. But don't make a sound. You don't want to get caught because then I'll have to share. And Daddy hates sharing."

I can't help it. As my lips close over the warm, silky smooth head of his dick, I also slide one hand along my drenched and swollen folds, stroking. Just for a second. Just until I realize I might get in trouble for it. But his words spark things inside of me, dark things that swirl and ache for release.

My jaw clamps tighter on Gunnar's dick as I force myself to focus only on him and wait my turn. Blading my tongue, I drag it over the underside of his cock and then swirl it around the head.

His hand comes down to fist in my hair and he lets me tease him, building up a rhythm.

I can't believe we're actually doing this. That he went along with it. And that he wants to pretend someone is still in here. Forcing myself to swallow down the moan I want to make around his cock is one of the hardest things I've ever had to do. Bill's murmurs drift into my head and I imagine that he's still here. That we're really being this blatantly naughty, that we're milliseconds away from getting caught.

My pussy is on fire.

My entire body is riddled with adrenaline and I'm nearly as mindlessly needy as when Gunnar edges me.

This kink of his is addictive in a dangerous way. My system is ticking like a countdown clock and I know it's only a matter of time before I implode. I press down further and take him deeper until his hand tugs my hair backward.

"On the desk." His tone is low and strained. Dangerous in a way I haven't heard before and I wonder if he's as affected as I am.

Probably.

I scramble out from underneath the desk clumsily, realizing that my legs are a tiny bit numb from being in that position. I stumble a little and, immediately, Gunnar's hands are at my waist, steadying me gently. Always there to catch me, even when he pushes me to the limit.

He helps me turn around and his eyes burn intensely as his fingertips dig in and he boosts me onto the top. My thighs immediately bracket his and my legs circle around him, cinching him closer, pulling him in, desperate to feel the press of his strength, his arms engulfing me, making me feel surrounded by his presence. He leans down, planting his hands on either side of me, the slight musk of his shaving cream hitting my nose. His breath is warm on my cheek as his lips ghost over the air just above my skin and he murmurs, "Take off my shirt."

His lips find my jawline and feather kisses over it, and as much as I want to just sink into the sensation, he's given me another order. Another task. I shakily search for my focus as my fingers find his buttons, undoing them one by one. Each inch of skin means I'm a tiny bit closer to my goal, to having him claim me here. In his space. In this other world we haven't yet entered together...this bubble we haven't popped. His job has been a separate entity, another hurdle to conquer. More judgment to face.

Does any of that really matter?

I used to think so. Used to worry about it even as I touched myself to thoughts of him.

I yank his shirttails roughly out of his pants, pulling his shirt wide and baring his abs and chest to my gaze. My eyes trail up over his firm body, the smattering of chest hair, the pulse pounding in his neck. And I wonder for a second, how I could ever worry about anything with him.

Meeting Gunnar was like stepping under the shelter of an umbrella during a storm. He's been my protector, my shield, my guard against all of the hell that life has rained down on me. Tears fill my eyes but I don't let them fall.

Instead, I feed that emotion into my touch as I reach up and drag my palms up over Gunnar's pecs, brushing gently over the tops of his nipples, dragging along his collarbone, up and down his neck, touching every bit of exposed skin I can, just reveling in the fact that he exists, that he's here---heart beating. And that he magically, miraculously loves me as much as I love him.

He nips at my jawbone, pulling me out of my emotional haze and back into the very naughty reality of our situation. I have no idea how long that bitch of a secretary comes back, but just like Daddy said he didn't like to share, I don't want to either. I don't even want her to get to hear his sounds of pleasure. So, I'd better stay focused. Resolved, I start pushing his shirt backward over his shoulders.

His lips leave my chin and he straightens, pulling his shirt off and then removing his pants, kicking them and his shoes off with an impatience that I'm certain is going to leave them a wrinkled mess. My orderly, demanding man is so impatient to have me that he's going to be an unmitigated disaster after this. God, I love that he's losing control.

"What now, Daddy?" I ask, eager to spur him on. With a little bit of daring that surprises me, I even spread my legs wider on the desk, fingers going down to pinch the hem of my skirt and play tauntingly with it.

"Lay back. I have something to teach you. But you're going to have to keep very still."

It takes every bit of willpower I have not to squeeze my thighs together as Gunnar gently reaches out and holds onto my back to help me lay across his desk. Once I'm down, he sits in his chair, the wheels drag slowly across his carpet as he rolls right up to me. Grabbing my legs one at a time, his fingers trail down my calves and lock around my ankles for a second as he plants my shoes on either armrest. Then he flips up my skirt so that it flaps down onto my belly and sends a gust of air at my face.

Nerves and delicious anticipation tangle me up.

"Oh, what a good girl. You're wet and ready for Daddy to play." His words stop and the next thing I feel is his hot breath against my seam a moment before his tongue darts out. The glide of that tongue liquifies my spine and all I can think of is fire. All I can feel is heat. My fingernails scratch at the desktop, searching for purchase. I end up reaching over-head and gripping the ledge of the desk.

He laps at me, a steady stroking pulse of wet warmth that could make me scream---if only he'd let me. Instead, I keep inhaling, harder and harder, filling up with air until I think my lungs might burst.

His fingers trace soft lines along my inner thighs as he continues to taste me, rhythmically but unhurried, very aware that he's torturing me in the most amazing way possi-ble. I imagine he's down there smiling, knowing how much control he's got over my body right now. But not just my body. Every part of me.

"Daddy, please let me cum," I beg in a soft whisper.

One of the fingers stroking up and down my thigh pauses, though his tongue keeps laving me gently. Then, that finger and its companions start trailing lines up my thigh, over my stomach, until his palm skates over the underside of my breast.

The combination of sensations makes me jerk my head and it smacks lightly against the desk. My mind is freefalling, cartwheeling and spinning through air, not held down by reality at all. I forget the rules, forget the stakes, forget everything except how amazing Gunnar makes me feel.

His fingers find my nipple. Pinch and twist.

I'm whirling.

Spinning past the moon.

His tongue plunges inside of me as his upper lip nudges harder against my clit.

There!

I writhe, pressing my heels into his chair, bucking and quivering, unable to control myself as my fingers clench down on the desk reflexively. Pleasure arcs through me in electric waves that are dizzying as he continues to twist my nipple and draw the sensation up from my core. It fills my chest and sets my heart racing.

Hazy and spent, my muscles unclench but the floating feeling doesn't leave me. It just grows less intense. I become boneless, sated but also starving for more. Content, but also alert and ready for whatever he's about to give me.

Gunnar rises, a smirk on his face before he smears my wetness from his lips with the back of his hand. "You were good and stayed quiet, Daisy."

"Do I get a reward for being good?"

He plants his hands on either side of me, a faux stern face ruined by the tiny smile that keeps tilting up the edge of his lips. "You already got a reward. Don't be greedy."

"But, I am." My fingers uncurl from the desk. They're sore as I reach for him but I don't care. I grab his shoulders and pull his chest into mine, needing to feel his body press against me. His warmth. The hard planes of him. I plant a soft kiss on his collarbone. I wrap my legs around his waist and tighten, drawing him in so that his length slides over me. "Spoil me, Daddy. You know you want to."

"Brat," he chuckles. But then he starts to grind against me, moving his hips in tiny circles. Dragging his dick just where I need it.

My arms loop around his neck and I pant against him as he pulls me back into that space of desperation. The way he can wring me out and control me, turn me from mischievous to enraptured in a few minutes---this man's a miracle.

"Oh! Oh!" I exclaim when he hits a spot that makes me start to quake.

"Not yet, little girl. You have to wait for me," Daddy immediately pulls back before lining himself up and plunging inside.

He just stole my pleasure!

But I don't even get a second to pout before he's holding me down on the desk and pounding into me. The snap of his hips feels loud. The quake of the desk. The slight drag of it against the carpet as daddy rails me in his office. Everyone's going to hear. They're all going to know---

The thrill of anxiety shoots me right over the edge and within seconds, I'm clamping down on Gunnar's cock, coming undone.

"Naughty, Daisy. I'll have to spank you for that later," Daddy's eyes gleam with anticipation but they're also glazed with lust.

He fucks me so hard my breasts are shaking, so hard a paper-weight falls from the corner of his desk onto the floor. And he doesn't stop. I don't think he could if he wanted to.

Not even if the door unlocked and someone walked in and we got caught.

"Think they can hear us outside?" I whisper. "Think they'll be able to smell sex in your office after you've come inside my pussy?"

His hands clamp down on my shoulders. If I thought he was fucking me hard before that was nothing. He slams into me. The smack is so intense that it knocks the breath from my lungs. But it's also fucking delicious.

Depraved.

Just like my Daddy.

With a groan that he buries in my neck, Gunnar comes, pulsing inside of me, dick tapping my inner walls. I hold him tight when he slumps into me, not surprised to find his torso has a slight sheen of sweat. After he's recovered enough to lift his head, he smiles gently down at me.

"Did I ever tell you that you're perfect?" he murmurs, before leaning down to give me a peck on the lips.

Butterflies start fluttering their wings inside of me. "Not sure."

"Well. You are."

He pushes himself up and slides gently out of me, glancing around for something to clean me up. He has to snag the box of tissues from the floor. I hadn't noticed them fall, but... I was focused on more important things.

Gunnar gently wipes me off before opening his desk drawer and retrieving my things. He pushes my hands back down whenever I lift them, saying, "I want to dress you."

So I let him. I let him try to smooth down my horribly wrinkled skirt. I let him struggle and chuckle as he tries to stick on the nipple pasties. They keep slipping off and after the fifth try he gives up, tossing them in the trash. I watch the way his pupils dilate as he stares at my breasts as he buttons up my blouse. As he gets and then carefully arranges my jacket to then hide them from view.

Once I'm clothed, I move to help him but he's too quick, checking his watch, eyes glancing toward the door. "I don't think she's back yet, but she will be soon." He mentions Melissa vaguely. "And I have one meeting I have to go to this afternoon. But..."

"But?" I scoop up his paperweight and put it back onto his desk for him. A desk that's now always going to remind me---and hopefully him---of today.

"If I come home early today, are you going to be home?"

"Where else would I be?"

He gives a shrug. "Out."

I take his hand and thread my fingers through his. "Nah. Out is lame. In's better."

"In is better. Deep inside you," he murmurs as we walk toward his door.

"Those are pretty dirty words for an old man. Need me to stop off for some little blue pills?" I tease.

A quick swat to my ass makes me give off a startled sound. But that quickly dissolves into a giggle.

"You'll get a real spanking later," Gunnar promises.

I turn to him, eyes twinkling. Heart glowing like a beautiful sunset. "I look forward to it." I lean up on my tiptoes and rub the tip of my nose lightly against his.

He steals a quick kiss.

Noise outside his door makes him step back, pulling his hand from mine and quickly flicking open the lock, pulling open the door.

Melissa's poised there, about to knock. Her expression instantly sours.

"Still here?" she remarks.

Her question rubs me the wrong way. Maybe it shouldn't. Maybe it was innocent. But it doesn't feel that way. Something about it makes me feel lesser. Judged. And a little bit angry because she's ruining the beautiful high that time with Gunnar gives me.

Or maybe it's just the fact that I want her to expect me to still be here. I want her, and everyone else to know that I *should* be here. That I belong here. With Gunnar.

And I want her to know that he belongs to me.

Maybe it's just me being territorial.

Maybe it's the fact that this thing between us has been a long time coming.

Maybe it's the fact that, even though I absolutely love Gunnar's sneaking kink, I don't want our relationship to consist of literal sneaking around.

Maybe it's because I'm proud to be with him. Thrilled even. Overwhelmed by gratitude. Undeserving. Grateful.

Tears edge up in the corners of my eyes but I blink them back as I stare at Melissa for a beat. Then I turn to Gunnar and grab his hand, weaving our fingers back together and lifting his hand to my lips. I place a single kiss there.

"Yes, I'm still here. Spending time with my boyfriend."

I let the word linger in the air.

Melissa's nostrils flare as if a skunk just sprayed her in the face.

Fuck her.

Fuck anyone who looks at us like that.

But Gunnar...oh Gunnar's smile is as bright as the blinding midday sun. "Most wonderful girlfriend of all time, isn't she?" he asks Melissa, without ever looking over at the witch. He's simply staring at me.

I hear a triple bell ringing in my head, like in boxing, whenever a match is over. I feel like I've just won. Like our declaration knocked Melissa out.

Everything about being with Gunnar feels like a victory. One that fate's gifted to me.

Sometimes, fate is a bastard who screws you over and steals away the people you love.

But sometimes, it gives you someone who will stand beside you through the misery and the heartache. Someone who will share your pain and walk beside you through the worst of the worst. Sometimes, you get your own guardian angel.

That's my Gunnar.

And I won't hide that I love him. I don't think I could if I tried.

Eyes misting, I give him a little smile as I unthread our fingers and take a step back. Even though I'm close to crying, I walk out of that office with a spring in my step. Because Gunnar's the reason I'm looking forward to this afternoon. To tomorrow. And the day after that.

Gunnar's my reason for everything.

READ BOOK 2 NOW!

Blurb

ANGELO

Rose makes me blind with lust, but also with fury.

She's going to give me what I want, even if I have to black-mail her to get it.

She can hate me 'til her dying day, but I will not let this secret of hers stand.

I'm going to find out who hurt her … and show them they can't touch what's mine.

ROSE

He's crossed a line that we can't come back from.

Threatening to ruin my family is unforgivable.

I don't care about the crush I used to have on him, or the fact that he's my brother's best friend.

Angelo Walker is the devil incarnate.

And I refuse to bow to a demon … no matter how he tempts me.

Preorder Book 2 - Bedding Rose - Now!

AFTERWORD

If you're desperate for Rose's story, it's next...

Thank you times a bazillion for reading!

I hope I made your day just a little bit naughtier and more exciting. Thank you from the bottom of my heart for supporting my dream of corrupting minds like yours with book boyfriends who are better than reality.

If you need more dark romance, check out my Feral Princess series. It is an omegaverse shifter story with dub-con and tons of heat.

Please consider reviewing this lil read before you go so that other people can come in forewarned about how evil I am. I mean, you have a duty to your fellow readers, right?

Kisses,

Ann

ACKNOWLEDGMENTS

To the hubby who inspires me and helps me format every single one of these suckers, thank you. I'd never have written without your support.

Thanks to RK and Ivy for being the best friends ever and being my safe space for my chaos. Thank you to Colette for talking me through this insane attempt at contemporary. Thank you Lori for not bleaching out your eyes. Thanks to Candace for your honesty. Thanks to my cover designer, Sylvia, at Book Brander Boutique, for the lovely covers.

And thank you to all my readers who trust me to give you a good experience even when I genre hop. You're an amazing group and I'm so happy to have found you.

ALSO BY ANN DENTON

Choose from books on the following pages based on your current reading mood.

The standalone or the first book in each series are listed by mood. The darkest reads appear first and grow progressively more light-hearted so it makes it easy to find just what you're looking for next. I also tried to add some basic mood info at the bottom of each series page for you.

FERAL PRINCESS SERIES
(Completed Trilogy)

A hot, dark shifter omegaverse with dub con, a steamy alpha, a loving beta, and a sassy omega who thought she was going to be an alpha female. She was sooo wrong, but when she's claimed by the pack alpha, make no mistake, she has something to say about it.

Defiant - Book 1

Mood - #DARK #DIRTY #ALPHA

TANGLED CROWNS SERIES
(Completed Trilogy and spinoff in progress)

A medium-burn, medieval fantasy romance with a reluctant princess, the knights she jilted at the alter, and an enemies to lovers story that weaves laughter and tears together along with a plot to save the kingdom. (Reverse Harem)

Knightfall - Book 1

Mood - #BANTER #REDEMPTION
#WHAATJUSTHAPPENED

PINNACLE SERIES
(Completed Duet)

A medium-burn paranormal romance about a girl who gets herself sent to a reform academy on purpose, so she can recruit criminally-minded guys to pull off the magical heist of the century. (Reverse Harem)

Magical Academy for Delinquents #MAD - Book 1

Mood - #BADASS #FUN #SEXY GAMES

LOTTO LOVE SERIES
(Completed Duet)

A medium-burn, contemporary romantic comedy reverse harem about winning the lotto and doing whatever the hell you want with it, even if that means holding a Bachelorette-style competition for an entire harem of hotties.

Lotto Men - Book 1

Mood- #LOL #BLUSHING #NO WAY

RUBY - JEWELS CAFE SERIES
(Standalone)

A medium-burn, fated mates reverse harem with an angel on her last strike, some nerds and a tech demon determined to help her, and Christmas miracles.

Ruby

Mood - #SWEET #AWWW #GIGGLES

DARK TEMPTATIONS SERIES
(Incomplete)

A fast-burn monster reverse harem in an alternate reality where monsters rule the earth. A human woman is captured and auctioned off to the Four Terrors who will haunt her nightmares and her dreams alike.
Cowrite with Katie May.

Ravaged by Monsters - Book 1

Mood - #DARK #FATED LOVE
#WILD SEXY TIMES

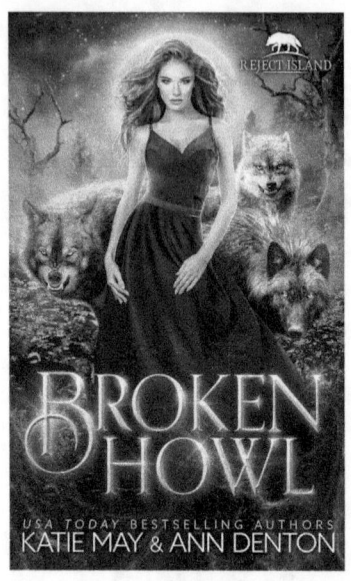

BROKEN HOWL
(Standalone)

A female omega rejects her mates so she can escape her abuser. She's sent to an island for rejects but her mates refuse to let her go…
Cowrite with Katie May.

Broken Howl

Mood - #CRYING #HEALING #FIGHTING

Darkest Queen Series
(Incomplete)

The devil is a woman. And this is the story about she fell from Heaven only to rise as God's greatest enemy... (A reverse harem spinoff of the Darkest Flames series) Cowrite with Katie May.

For Whom the Bell Tolls - Book 1

Mood - #FURY #SOUL-DEEP CONNECTIONS #BATTLE OF WILLS

DARKEST FLAMES SERIES
(Completed Trilogy with a novella)

A medium-burn paranormal romance about a girl who tries a love spell on the hot guy at school and accidentally summons demons instead. It contains psychotic, alpha males, and student/teacher relationships. (Reverse Harem) Cowrite with Katie May.

Demon Kissed - Book 1

Mood - #OOPS #NAUGHTY LAUGHTER #FORBIDDEN HEAT

DEMON'S JOY
(Standalone)

Santa's daughter has to save Christmas from demons! And all she's got to help her are five funny reindeer. (A reverse harem spinoff of the Darkest Flames series)
Cowrite with Katie May.

Demon's Joy

Mood - #SILLY #HOLIDAY CHEER #YUM

MAGE SHIFTER WAR SERIES
(Completed Duet)

A medium-burn paranormal mafia romance. A fae princess
is taken captive by three shifter criminals. (Reverse Harem)
Cowritten with Elle Middaugh.

Fae Captive - Book 1

Mood - #BONNIE&CLYDE #BADASS #HOT

HAMMER TIME
(Standalone)

A medium-burn paranormal comedy featuring Thor's daughter and a quest to save demigods from prison. Expect lots of ancient deities and potty humor. (Reverse Harem) Cowritten with M.J. Marstens.

Hammer Time

Mood- #PUNTASTIC #NOYOUDIDN'T #SNORT

CONNECT AND GET SNEAK PEEKS

Do you want to read exclusive point of views from different characters, make predictions and claim your book boyfriends with other readers, see my inspiration for these books, and hang with fellow romance lovers? Then join my Facebook Reader Group! I promise you'll love it!

Join Ann Denton's Reader Group

Facebook.com/groups/AnnDentonReaderGroup

ABOUT ME

I'm a shy lady who has always been obsessed with reading, travel, and live theater. I've lived in five states and currently reside in Maryland.

I have two of the world's cutest children, a crazy dog who licks the fridge obsessively, and an amazing husband who is my total opposite.